Departures

Departures

BRIAN LEYDEN
DEPARTURES

BRANDON

First published in 1992
as a paperback original
by Brandon Book Publishers Ltd,
Dingle, Co. Kerry, Ireland.

"The Last Mining Village" first appeared on RTE Radio 1 (1988)
and was published in *Force 10* magazine (1989); "Departures" on
BBC Radio 4 (1990) and *Force 10* (1990); "On the Market" on BBC
Radio 4 (1990); "Last Remains" in *Force 10* (1991); "New Islands"
in *Stet* magazine (1992).

British Library Cataloguing in Publication Data
Leyden, Brian
  Departures
  I. Title
  823.914 [FS]

  ISBN 0 86322 154 8

This book is published with the financial assistance of the Arts
Council/An Chomhairle Ealaíon, Ireland.

Cover design: The Graphiconies (Foreman)
Front cover photograph: Thomas Quinn
Internal design and typesetting: Brandon
Printed by Colourbooks, Dublin

To my mother and father

Contents

The Last Mining Village

THEY SAID THE COAL MINES would not last much
longer. And it seemed, with every passing week,
another one of the old characters had gone to
that dauby graveyard on the hill.

Picture a valley by a lake below an iron- and rusty-red
mountain. Add a pub, a parish hall, two grocers' shops,
scattered housing, a bridge, a river and a loose knot of
coal-and-oil-black roads.

On Easter Sunday morning outside an immaculate
church, bright as the pearly gates, gleaming lines of family cars grace the carpark below the church and graveyard. A church bell tolls, calling the respectable,
responsible citizens of the valley to mass. A late-comer
trips up the steps, creaks and bangs the door, turns all
heads, and slips, shamefaced, into a seat at the back.
Then the hushed and prosperous Sunday morning stillness.

Dark figures shuffle in the church porch. They crouch
and whisper over the prayers, sermon, coughs and bells
of the mass going on inside. They talk about coal mines,

cattle and current affairs.

"I hear the Germans bought a farm over on the far mountain."

"You don't buy a farm over there, you buy an address."

The sun breaks through the stained-glass windows above the altar and scatters like confetti across the aisle. It is after half-past eleven. The men outside listen for sounds of the crowd stirring.

"Go forth in peace."

"Amen."

And the race is on. The shopkeeper's assistant is out the door like a shot off a shovel. A quick blessing and they pour out the church door like dark treacle running down the steps. Engines throb to life, misty exhausts fume in the carpark. Men and women and children bolt down the road with unbuttoned best coats. The clicking and clacking of high heels kicking up the gravel and dry leaves under a chestnut tree as old as the valley. It is neck and neck all the way to the paper-seller's hut.

And then they're off again, with a near-naked and brazen huzzy tucked under one arm on the front page of the *Sunday World*: naughty and giggling with a promising of scandal, Fr Brian D'Arcy and the cartoons.

The finishing post is an always-open-on-Sundays shop where the crowd will always be there before you. Women with Sunday dinners on their minds, lined six-deep at the counter. Calling for freshly roasted chickens, frozen peas, carrots, cauliflower and ice-cream, litres of lemonade, sweet cakes and something for the supper. And treats for scrubbed children on their Sunday best behaviour.

Outside, patient men in long coats and white, open-neck shirts shuffle around the pub door, like the mourners of Lazarus waiting for the miraculous opening of the tomb. What do they care about the black-coat-and-hat brigade of pious tooth-suckers, tut-tutting as they pass, swallowing eucharist and gossip between lips as severe as a Good Friday collation.

With righteous heads held high they aim their sharp, viper tongues at a certain big redheaded, loud-laughing, pint-loving lout sporting an outlawed Easter lily, sideburns, cowboy boots and baggy trousers from a mart-day stall.

"He didn't get that head drinking spring water."

The easy Sunday babble of the river follows the good people walking home from mass. In the pub the Sunday drinkers discuss work, jobs, money and the future. Over the rim of the frosted glass in the bar-room window, heaps of wet coal glitter on the dark hill overlooking the pub.

"There's a race of men that don't fit in
They'd break the heart of kith and kin
They'd break the heart of a stone
Break the heart of a stone."

The big man whispers into his drink. But nobody is listening.

Establish your credentials here with a pint. And sitting at the bar, overhear a yarn about Francie the barber, who lived by the church and shaved the priest for beer-money.

"Do you remember the morning Francie got the shakes and he drew blood with the old cut-throat razor? And the priest said:

"'That's the drink for you, Francie.'

"'I know, Father, it leaves the skin very tender.'"

The ganger Gaffney adds to the legend, and he tells the company about the time the same priest was walking back to his house after saying mass when he met Francie, staggering past the chapel, on his way home from the pub.

"'I'm warning you now, Francie, you're on the very brink of hell.'

"'Didn't they build it very close to the church, Father?'"

Outside, the shrill yelps of children. Out of nowhere the travelling fair has arrived. Each year it comes mysteriously, like the first snow. Brightly painted and always harbouring some dark secret behind the painted shutters. And always a mad dog chained at the back of the slumbering caravans. The children haggle for silver from their parents and mount the rides with rough glee. Screams of delight pierce the brittle air. All is harmless now in the hard light of day. It will only develop its special, sinister magic when darkness falls. When the fairground music echoes the length of the valley and the whir and clatter of the rides mingle with boisterous shouts of young and old. When the blue dusk falls like magic powder on the eternal fairground and restores to life swing-boats, rifle-ranges, bumper-cars, and a childlike sense of wonder.

Once upon a time hard men walked the valley. Those were the days of gang fights, Paisley shirts and broad ties, purple suits with matching waistcoats, bell-bottom trousers and platform shoes. After a week of hacking deep in the belly of the mountain the weekends were given over to drinking and fighting. To days of long-standing rivalry between the country dance-halls that served nothing stronger than minerals and bags of cheese-and-onion crisps.

Long lines of Honda fifties – twenty-five or more – circled the village in clouds of summer dust, and then trailed off to a neighbouring parish. Looking for trouble and usually finding it: fist-fights and broken furniture, torn jackets, blood on white shirt-fronts. Split lips, bleeding noses.

Or drinking all day before a feed of burgers and white

soup at the chipper, and then on to the Mayflower ball-room. To hear Joe Dolan or Margo or Big Tom.

The crowded cloakrooms, the empty dance-floors. Girls dancing together – steps rehearsed at home or in school corridors; long lines of girls sitting with their backs to the wall.

And the crush: that body of youths milling close to the sweaty walls, tightly packed, like prisoners chained to the pillar, going round and round asking every girl in the line for a dance.

"Will you come for a slither on the boards?"

"Will you lean up against me for this one?"

"Would you ever hold me pint, I'm bursting for a ..."

"No No No."

And then, of course, there was always the village bike. A big-hearted, broad-hipped girl, engaged more often than the women's toilets at Connolly station. But never married. Like that last turkey on the supermarket shelf; everybody had a squeeze but nobody took her home.

In the slippery, wet-floored, reeking toilets the young men slick back their hair before returning to the crush to try their luck or, perhaps, their looks again. And standing at the urinal you hear a low, serious conversation. Two boys with slurred voices face one another.

In the wink of an eye one goes down. Blink and you miss that smart smack to the jaw, that gush of blood from a burst lip, that sudden buckling at the knees before he slumps to the floor.

One man lies stretched and another man with bruised knuckles and dead eyes, breathing beer and onions, leans up against you and says:

"He was asking for that."

And you'd be a fool to disagree.

There was always more action at the door, where the trouble with the bouncers started. Big men, like sides of meat with bow-ties on, who always seemed to be looking for a fight. And you could look on at the minor scuffles among the colliers and doormen and recall one mad, full-moon night when the ballroom came under siege.

Stones were thrown through windows and the bouncers kneeled under the broken panes like cowboys cornered in a western saloon. Then somebody tossed a motorbike through the window. A red and white Honda fifty crash-landed on the dance-floor and the bouncers fled for home. Chased all the way to the county border by youths yelling abuse out the windows of Ford cars.

Cars were made for cowboys then. The bog-standard old Ford Escort, with extra-heavy springs in the back. And the king of cars, the mark two Cortina E in chrome and black, with furry dice, simulated leopard-skin seat covers, a cassette player warbling country music and a cardboard air-freshener with a naked girl hanging from the rear-view mirror. Back seat romances, reclining front seats and smoochy music. How many girls stepped into marriage through the passenger doors of those second-hand cars?

After every summer there were casualties. Hurried marriages before it showed. And on and on it goes: long after the furtive encounters at the backs of dance-halls, long after the passing of the ballroom days the romance, the bouncing springs, the steamed-up windows remain. In hotel carparks where the discos are the new kings crowned with coloured spotlights. A new generation is born, but habits remain the same. Second-hand cars, dances, fights and childhood codes of honour.

"Eggs and rashers for the Arigna smashers,

Hay and oats for the Drumshanbo goats."

And then, shortly after that first shave with his father's razor, he drops his school bag for a pit helmet, and the promise of freedom bought with a working man's wage.

The pit lorry passes the school bus and a pale-faced student looks over at black, grimy-faced pals: tired but suddenly grown-up men in tattered working clothes, working off a bellyful of last night's porter.

"What does your father do?"

"He works in the power-station."

"Shovelling light into dark corners."

Memories of innocence before hard labour. Before adult rites of passage in the dark mines and bars. And a question for a bystander:

"You never worked in the pits yourself?"

"I'll be long enough underground."

We have all gone our own ways now. But we remember common ground.

The national school was built three miles away from the village centre; as the pitmen headed to work the scholars set out for school. Walking the long road to a day in school whose only reward was the journey home. A journey past hay-barns and orchards. Orchards with sour green crab-apples that tasted like nectar, protected by a notice saying "Trespassers Will Be Prosecuted". And still you dared, and you had to reach through the mossy branches for the reddest, sweetest apple that was, always, at the top of the tree.

On the way home "Poodle" Dean drank water from the puddles and ate earthworms for a dare. And everybody stamped on the hosts of flying ants, because you never forgave them for their stings, years ago, when you sat on their nests by accident in short trousers, and found your pants full of pismires.

But it is all changing so fast. New schools and new open cast mines. In the old days they sank mine-shafts here. Tunnelled their way to the seams of coal. The men marched underground, a hundred or more working in one mine. Foreheads lit by pale flames from brassy, bubbling carbide-and-water lamps hanging on their helmets. Swallowed up each morning by the open mouth of the pit. Only a glimmering thread of lights leading in to their private, subterranean world. And a long steel cable fishing out lines of hutches. Rattling out on narrow rails, and loaded with shiny, black lumps of coal.

The lorries, painted red then, rumbled down the valley and rattled back empty from the habitually smoking power-station with its tall chimney like a balanced cigarette, on Lough Allen's shore. Above the noise of conveyor belts, pumps and air compressors came the screech of the sawmill, where pillars and props – that would soon be creaking and bending under the dripping wet weight of the mountain – were cut. But no more.

The old mines are closing. Slowly turning to places of ghosts and memories. The wealth of coal exhausted. The old shafts have been sealed up and regiments of conifers press in on these abandoned places. Graveyards marked with mechanical headstones. It would take a child or an artist to find beauty now in places so full of rain, rust and ruin. Among the tangled remains of broken hutch-wheels. Among fallen-down sheds and shattered windows and broken rails. Among rusty, serpent-coils of steel rope and bent pipes scattered to the wind like drinking straws. Among the ghost voices of long dead men and their fiercely guarded ways.

The Sunday drinkers are having one for the road; the yarns are all told, the painted shutters are going up on the fairground booths. Dinners and papers, wives and children, the Sunday football game and the afternoon snooze are waiting amongst the bungalows. And far from schoolhouses and dance-halls, far from fairgrounds and bars, far from scandals and prayers, far from pits and power-station, the road takes me away from a valley by a lake below a mountain.

A Good One

I T WAS A TIME WHEN only a *bona fide* traveller could
buy drink on a Sunday. And the bicycle riding constabulary, using white imperial measuring tapes on
spools that were made to read the width of the road at
the scenes of traffic accidents and collisions, took the
measure of the journey from your front doorstep to the
brass foot-rail of the bar counter. Less than three miles
between the two locations and you had no legal right to
spring the arm of the bell over the door of a drinking
premises, nor leave your money down on the wood.

The last Sunday in the month of July, Garland Sunday.
A day, by tradition, when good people went to mass up
in the mountains. A day when country priests stood over
lichen-circled mass rocks in the heather, and the worship-
pers made Sunday outings along the bracken paths to
gather on the breezy crests of the summer hills. A day
when more adventurous pilgrims brought sturdy sticks
for the reek, and went barefoot and fasting up the scree
paths and slopes of the holy mountain, Croagh Patrick.

John Hubert is up an hour when he feels his famous

thirst bettering his devotion. With the split sections of a traditional wooden flute, locally known as his three-piece wallet, snug in the inside pocket of his good suit jacket he walks the mile or so into town looking for a *seisiún*. He meets a crowd of people on the sunny pavement and stops to talk to a pilgrim neighbour, queuing for the bus for Croagh Patrick. Then he crosses the street to Murray's public house and walks casually past the front door, double-bolted between the holy hours from two until four o'clock. He goes around to a brown side-door with the words Wines and Spirits printed in gold leaf on the narrow pane of glass above the lintel.

"John Hubert," says a blue-uniformed sergeant, appearing out of the shadowy door of the whitewash and Rickett's blue outhouse, where the publican kept his winter turf and bottled and corked his stout out of the brewery kegs. "Are you not going to the reek today?"

"No," says John Hubert. "But I was going to knock."

Last Remains

MRS MCDAID ALWAYS SAT IN the kitchen in an armchair, smoked dark brown by the open fire. Reading religious magazines with names like *The Sacred Heart* and *The African Mission, The Far East* and *The Messsenger*. She was my granny, and people said she was a very pious woman. I was afraid of her.

We lived only a short distance down the road from my grandparents then. And each evening I had to fetch a sweet-can full of hot, frothy milk from the farm. I always avoided the kitchen window, going down the cobbled back-yard directly to the barn where Tom McDaid did the milking.

If I came early I would help Tom by driving in the cattle. He would wait in the yard, searching the clouds at the butt of the hill for tomorrow's weather. With savage shouts I would bluster and threaten the rheumatic cattle: "come-up-out-of-that," who came trudging and creaking through the rushes at their own pace, spattering my bare legs with cow-dung.

When the cattle were tied at their stakes I stood in the

doorway teasing flakes of whitewash from the stone walls. The barn was big, warm and thatched with generations of cobwebs woven through the rafters. I listened to the splish-splash regular rhythm, as his two strong hands drew white strokes from the swollen udders into a galvanised iron bucket. When he finished he dipped his finger into the froth on the milk and drew a cross on the cow's flank. The cow chewed away like the old woman of the house.

Granny McDaid came out to strain the milk through a square of muslin, measuring out my three pints with great exactness. She hobbled about on arthritic legs and a bad hip, supported by an evil-looking blackthorn walking stick.

"Off with you now, before it gets dark," she would gesture with her stick. "Before the pookey man gets you."

Thursday was churning day. Mrs McDaid stood over the wooden butter churn in the flagstone-floored outhouse Tom called the dairy. Tom and myself fetched and carried for her. Running with kettles of scalding water, or carrying between us the big black and red earthenware crocks, with smooth lids of clotted cream.

Mrs McDaid operated the dash, her mottled hands gripping the long handle going through the lid of the barrel-shaped churn. Tom had made that dash at his bench in the cart-shed where he kept his oilstones, handsaws, spokeshave, spirit level, chisels and blades in bright order, and cut the magic pattern through which the old woman pumped the milk into butter.

"Bad cess to it, it doesn't make proper butter," she would up-cast to him.

Then she called for more hot water, with her red-rimmed eyes on the thermometer in its wooden jacket. Finally, I ran for cups to taste the buttermilk, rags to wipe the lid, salt and strainer. We gazed into the pungent depths of the churn and looked down on the pale clots of butter floating on the steaming milk or stuck to the grain in the sides of the wooden churn.

I was reared on the taste of Blue Band margarine and I hated the taste of that colourless and salty country butter which the old woman patted into ovals with her wrinkly hands.

Though the butter tasted disgusting and though I was always getting things wrong, or being told to get out from under the old woman's feet, I never missed churning day. For each time the lid of the churn was raised that purest sense of wonder struck as the miracle of the making of the butter was revealed.

Every Friday evening I brought the milk money to Mrs McDaid. I dreaded the evenings I didn't have the exact change. Then I would have to help the old woman up the stairs to her bedroom. A room which was always locked. She kept the key on the end of a shoe-lace which was pinned somewhere inside the many folds and layers of her cardigans and skirts.

I would stand by the door as the lock clicked and she heaved herself up the last step into the sinister bedroom. After a long wait I sometimes worked up the courage to steal a glimpse of the room. There was a heavy wooden crucifix nailed up on the wall over her candlewick bedspread, ringed by pictures and prints of jaundice-yellow and gloomy apostles. More saints and wounded martyrs watched over a big wardrobe stuffed with coats and dresses from Yankee parcels. There was a dressing table smothered in bottles and holy water vessels, medications, tablets, ointments and rubs. The room smelt of camphor and mothballs, holy candles, medicine and her.

I waited as she rustled and poked through the top

drawer of her dressing table, sifting big, old-money paper notes; fire-brick red ten-shilling notes, green pounds with the picture of the woman with the harp on the front, and huge notes with river gods on the back, in rainbow shades of mauve and blue.

My eyes fell to the floor again when she came hobbling out with the change. Unlike Tom she never offered me a couple of age-blackened halfpennys, or a big brown penny the full size of my fist for an expedition to the shop for bull's-eyes, penny biscuits or a lucky bag.

With the proper change in an envelope in my pocket, safely sealed and addressed to my mother, I had to link her down the stairs again. The old woman always came down steps and stairs backways. Clinging to the banisters on one side and me on the other. I suffered her weight and her cold touch and the smell of Vick's ointment and waited with her each time she told me she had to stop to "rift gas".

On Sunday mornings Granny McDaid arranged for a hackney man to bring everybody to first mass. Escorted by Tom on one side and my father on the other, wearing her pearl-brooched and best black coat, Yankee bonnet and veil, she led the procession of neighbours up the length of the church and took her proper place in the varnished front seat with the padded kneeling board.

I would sit fidgeting by her side, while Mrs McDaid mouthed her prayers, always a full blessing ahead of the priest. Having suffered the compulsory fast before communion, the smell of rashers on the pan and Denny's pork sausages dipped in a soft fried egg invaded my nostrils, in anticipation of the ritual fry for Sunday breakfast waiting in our warm kitchen at home. The mass seemed to last an eternity and afterwards we had to wait for Mrs McDaid to finish her private chat with the priest and the darling altar boys.

Canon Daly, a man feared by every school-going or mitching child in the half-parish, came to visit Mrs McDaid's house on the first Friday of every month. Confessions were heard and rumours exchanged. From these talks with both parish priest and canon, together with the gossip gathered every Saturday on her visits to the medical dispensary, she knew that the entire village was a hotbed of heedless spending and ungodly appetites.

Every first Friday after the canon left I would sit and listen to her giving out about "that trollop" who stood behind the village bar. And then she sucked her teeth over the sinful sums of money taken in across the glass-bottom-ringed counter from those shameless slaves to Arthur Guinness.

When I got home my mother would send me to the pub to ask Tom and my father if they were ready to come home. A mission which always involved a wait on a high padded seat in the smokey front bar, rewarded with a mineral and a bag of crisps as another round of pints mysteriously appeared.

On Friday mornings Tom always sat in the square of light close to the kitchen window, his elbows resting on the oilcloth, while Mrs McDaid sat in her chair by the fire calling out her wants: Andrews liver salts, baking soda, Fry's cocoa, Birds's custard, Fiery Jack's liniment, sugar – in case of another shortage – and a half-quarter of tobacco, which was Tom's reward.

Then she would stop to make up the prices in her head, her idea being that the total bill for the shopping should leave Tom without the price of a drink. At the same time the bill should not be too great. Then the balance would have to be taken out of her own pension money.

Tom's only defence was to keep the bit of paper on which the list was written very small. He quartered an already tiny sheet of paper taken from an airmail writing pad, using his oiled and surgically sharp pocket-knife. Then he fished out the shiny metal case where he kept his spectacles and a stubby blue pencil. After teasing the wire frames around his ears he scraped a needle point on the pencil to copy each item down in his neat, meticulous handwriting.

Granny McDaid took a long time before calling out each article as she added up the prices under her breath. When she finally lapsed into silence Tom folded up his square of paper, put away the end of pencil, and tucked the list neatly in under his glasses in the silver case, which he deposited in the inside pocket of his second-best jacket, the one with the leatherette patches on the elbows. Mrs McDaid, having decided that the total bill was still less than Tom's entire pension money, then called out another item.

"Can't you leave it at that woman? There's no room on the list."

"Well, get another bit of paper, you old fool."

Tom might have put away the spectacle-case five or six times and have as many separate scraps of paper with additions to the original list before Granny fetched their pension books from the dressing table upstairs, to add her official signature. And, somehow, Mrs McDaid always got her sums wrong and Tom could be found every Friday evening in the pub singing like a blackbird on an apple branch.

By the time my mother would have given the order to fetch Tom and my father home from the public house a crowd would have gathered around old Tom McDaid. The company was lively because Tom always had a puzzle, a riddle or a mathematics problem. He had a fresh problem every week, and for these his audience divided into two camps. The one camp, usually led by my father, gave him a fair hearing, pausing over their pints to puzzle out Tom's new conundrum.

"There's more ways to kill a cat than choke him with butter," Tom would announce, after every wrong answer.

A pub regular in wellingtons, by the name of Pat Michael, with a full company of bar-rail supporters, acted fool in the middle. After Pat Michael volunteered a particularly stupid answer Tom would wheel around and inform him: "The hens in our yard have more brains."

On a second attempt he might add: "If you said that to our ass, he'd kick you."

But the good boys were only happy with the evening if they led old Tom to dance on his hat with frustration. Then the woman from behind the bar settled the argument, spun the green-lit wireless dial to Athlone, and took Tom out for an old-time waltz until it was time to go home.

Tom always arrived back merry and red-faced, and in good appetite for his favourite boiled flat Dutch cabbage, bacon marbled with fat and soda-bread plastered with salty home-made butter. Mrs McDaid waited on him, her plan of attack postponed by the sight of her proper pension money and the groceries, which had been delivered earlier by the shop van, all present and in order. Finally, she took to her chair by the fire, severe but silent, sipping her liver salts.

She had to wait for the next day to launch her attack. On Saturdays Tom stretched himself on the brown, wooden settle-bed in the kitchen corner, his hat down over his eyes, his head in his hands, and no man at death's door ever moaned louder or felt more sorry for himself.

And then, one stiff and grey winter Saturday, Mrs McDaid headed for the medical dispensary in a hired car, a trip she made, hail or ailing, every Saturday of the year. When the doctor had finished his examination, and had given her two kinds of tablets, he left, as usual, by the back door. Mrs McDaid returned to an empty waiting room, with no sign of the hackney man outside. Pat Michael and a neighbour found her stranded in the porch.

"You can't stay there, Mrs McDaid. Come on with us. We'll link you as far as the pub. You can sit at the fire while we ring for another hackney man."

The roads were icy, the wind bitterly cold. Mrs McDaid consented, and the two men linked her to the public house.

"You'll have a hot one with us? A whiskey, Mrs McDaid, with hot water, a pinch of sugar and a few cloves. Sure, it'll take the chill out of your bones."

It was a bitterly cold day and she had been waiting a long time. She drank the hot whiskey down and Pat Michael went to the bar for another. Some people said she just took a bad turn, but most agreed afterwards it was the strong spirits combined with the tablets she had taken such a short time before that killed her.

"The Lord between us and all harm," said Pat Michael, catching her as she fell.

And for years to come, whenever Pat Michael got very drunk he would say: "She died in me arms, God rest her. Right in that very spot," pointing towards the seat under the window engraved with the legend, "Powers Whiskey".

I was on the front street, watching Tom pull a length of string through a ball of pitch to make a sort of cobbler's thread he called waxend, when the procession arrived from the village. They carried the remains into the front parlour and then they brought down Tom's settle-bed from the kitchen and left her out on that until the room upstairs was ready. Two neighbouring women were sent for to see to the corpse. Pat Michael carried water for them.

When Mrs McDaid was laid out properly in her own room, I crept in to see her. The women had fitted a shroud with a holy picture on her chest under her crossed hands. They had combed back her hair. There was a Bible and a wedge of tissue under her chin to keep the mouth closed. And a black rosary beads threaded through her fingers.

With the door closed the noise of the callers downstairs seemed very distant and the air in the room thick with silence. The curtains were drawn: the only light came from two blessed candles alongside the silver crucifix with the round base that was only taken out for a station in the house.

I had never seen a dead person before. My mind could not grasp the depth of silence that surrounded the corpse, the perfect stillness and the utter absence of all the things that had made Granny McDaid such a fearful old woman.

Mrs McDaid had died in a crowded pub on a Saturday afternoon. News spread fast and wide. A crowd of people had already gathered in the McDaid house, the number swelling fast with a constant stream of callers coming in ones and twos and hushed parties of four.

Two old sisters of Mrs McDaid met the people inside the door. Pat Michael was dispatched to the pub, taking me along with him for the spin. The first job was to buy drink for the wake. His order was generous, being funded from the rustling top-drawer of Mrs McDaid's dressing table. He loaded the hackney man's old Ford with boxes of shopping, extra bread and rattling cases of drink until there was scarcely enough room for the driver and himself, with me sitting on the handbrake.

We visited the undertaker next to order the casket, phone the times of the removal and the funeral to the papers, and to arrange the marking out of the plot where the neighbouring men would dig the grave in turns.

The winding clock over the fireplace was put away when the corpse was brought into the house. The early winter evening fell with the McDaid sisters passing out pipe-to-bacco and saucers filled with cigarettes, and every caller was met with a drink.

Big-bosomed women bedecked in black, with bottles of porter, naggins of whiskey, steaming teapots, ham sandwiches, home-made currant cake, blessed candles and bottle openers, milk jugs, sugar bowls, and trembling grips that were a danger to my mother's good china, were bossily in charge for the night.

By midnight there was broken glass on the kitchen floor where bottles had fallen over and the flagstones were slippery with treacle-black stout. A crowd of people lined the stairs where spilt beer ran from step to step. Men clutching whiskey bottles told the funniest and the oldest yarns of great characters long dead. Distant relatives appeared. Fighting neighbours shook hands. And old Tom was settled quietly in a corner. It was my job to look after him, but he didn't move or say a word all night.

"She'd never have approved of the drinking," said Pat Michael, throwing back a half-one with his little finger in the air, "but it's a grand wake all the same."

"I'm thinking we won't see the likes of it again in our time," said another pub stalwart. "God be with the old wakes, when there was music in the kitchen and match-making in the hall, and a cow turned out of the barn for a tumble in the warm spot."

"I won't stand for that kind of talk under this roof," said Pat Michael. "She was a decent woman, God rest her. One of the old sort."

"Lord have mercy," they said in unison.

It was long past my bedtime when the old women arranged for a rosary to be said over the corpse before the family moved in to keep their night vigil. I pushed my way up through the crowd on the stairs and went into the bedroom, where I knelt next to the door as the old women called out their sorrowful mysteries.

When the rosary was said several of the late callers placed their hands lightly over the hands of the corpse before quitting the room. Pat Michael was standing behind me. He prodded me in the back.

"Touch the corpse," he said.

I was still stunned by her passing, and by the sight of that pale form lying there between the cold, white cotton sheets. As I crossed the room I was dimly aware that I was a witness to the passing of a hard-won, self-sufficient world. Witness to the passing of the last remains of brown wooden settle-beds and barrel butter churns, winding pocket watches and guessing at the weather from the front street, Yankee dresses and parcels, sixpenny bits and florins, old women ramblers and callers to the well for water, late night card-games and ghost stories told by the fire, with sworn sightings of will-o'-the-wisps and the wandering dead.

I reached out my hand, then took it back quickly. Her skin had the same cold wax feel as a church candle. Pat Michael nodded, and then ushered me out of the room. With his hand left on my shoulder he said: "You have to touch the corpse, or you'll dream about her tonight."

Christmas Promise

T HE DAY AFTER WE GOT the Christmas holidays we took the bus to a crowded shopping town with my mother. Her lists made out, the money carefully rolled in a big black purse with a brass clip, she walked us to the crossroads in our nylon anoraks. There was an excited hurry in our step as we trotted a country mile to the main road. My younger brother swinging his arms to keep up the pace. My mother watching the time on a small gold wrist-watch. But we got there a few minutes early, our foreheads hot and our scalps tingling.

"It's not gone yet."

"That's if it's coming at all."

And we worried until we sighted the sun-flash of the driver's big windshield, the red and white coachwork lurching towards us, taking up most of the road and pulling up tight against the ditch as we came around the front to the open door. We stood on the step up as the driver searched a school exercise book with the fares written in blue biro. My mother with the right money ready in her fist.

Down the middle aisle we made our way, minding our paper tickets. Past a small man with his hands in his lap, smiling through plastic teeth. There were several more neighbours we knew by sight or by nickname: Kate the miller, long Tom, Pratie Gallagher, Pat the blower and Pat the twin. Small women in belted coats and printed cotton headscarves. Husbands wearing good suits and cardigans inside their jackets, with topcoats and felt hats, talking about airlocks and shorthorns.

"You're late on it today," my mother says to a neighbour, and they start to chat as soon as she takes her seat. Everyone who boards the bus is brought into the conversation.

"What have you all the coats for, Mary?"

"They were giving out rain on the radio."

"You're looking as fit as a fiddle, Jimmy."

"I could kiss me toes if I had me socks off."

Smooth-faced women with three chins and coiled barbed-wire-tight home perms holding fur-lined gloves, embroidered shopping bags and tied umbrellas, all gabbing together like market-day turkeys.

The bus made slow progress up through the gears but never made any speed. It was always delayed behind a slow car driven at twenty-five miles an hour by a little man looking out through the steering wheel. Or a tractor with baled hay and a bucket of calf-nuts in the transport box. Then we had to stop to leave the papers off at every post office. It was a full hour before we reached the blue outskirts of the town.

The town lights stayed lit all day in the deep gloom of December. We got off at the traffic lights on the Mail Coach road and took a short-cut into the centre. On the terraced hill above we saw men out in their gardens, smoking cigarettes and waiting for the shopping wives to come home. Chapel spires looming through the blanket of coal smoke and fog. The streets netted with coloured bulbs. Snow-capped cars down from the mountains.

"Where do you want to go first, Mammy?"

"We'll go to the hardware."

"Do you not want to shop for clothes?"

"Why don't we look in the Market Yard?"

Ringed close about our mother we stood to plot the day. She opened her purse and looked at her money again.

"We'll stay with you, Mammy, until you get the shopping done."

And we followed her about the shops, adding unwanted items to her shopping basket: cooking chocolate, apricots, walnuts.

"We don't need all that," Mammy would say. "And put that bottle back and get me a smaller one."

She kept us distracted roving the supermarket aisles finding items off her list: tin foil, brown sauce, packets of jelly, sponges for the trifle. But we didn't want to buy all our wants here, where, my mother said, they would stand over you looking for the last penny. The turkey, the ham, the bread and the milk and eggs and loose rashers we would need to tide us over the holiday when the shops were closed, we would get from the local shopkeeper, who always sent up an additional Christmas box of a cake and cigarettes with our order.

Between shops the Christmas shopping crowd elbowed and jostled around each other on the packed streets, everybody clutching a brace of plastic supermarket bags with dodgy bottoms, the sides worn ragged by the extra boxes of all shapes and sizes in bright wrapping paper. We saw small, shabby men in working clothes stagger home after Christmas drinks. Cotton wool-bearded Santies wearing black wellingtons, sitting in red crêpe paper-covered booths, with the shop charging for every visit. Plain women buying little presents for themselves. Loaded family cars, the children messing with the lights, parked outside the supermarkets. Perished young lads selling pine trees in the carpark corner. Tinker children selling holly. Seasonal biscuit boxes and tea-caddies, rich chocolate liqueurs, cards, clementines and tinsel decorations, fairy lights and snow sprayed from aerosol cans in the shop windows, latticed with red insulating tape. The enticements to spend were everywhere.

There are old people in from the country moving in twos: unmarried brothers and spinster sisters, giving out constantly amongst themselves, clearing a path with their sticks. And carol singers in the arcade, led by a bearded man with a guitar. Passing the rattling collectors' cans we have a coin and a recitation out of memory ready:

"Christmas is coming and the geese are getting fat
Will you please put a penny in the old man's hat
If you haven't got a penny, then a halfpenny will do
If you haven't got a halfpenny, then God bless you."

Chubby children in hooded coats run wild amongst the big, expensive toy displays. They open boxes, drag down stuffed toys, battery-driven and spring-wound things and leave them scattered about the shop floor.

"This is what Santy is bringing me," they shrill.

"If you don't behave Santy won't bring you anything. Now, come on."

We are taken into the toy department to pick out one special want; a book, a junior mechanical kit, an Airfix model aircraft or a chemistry set.

"They have me robbed," my mother says to a passing school-master.

"Anything that's educational," he says.

With our presents parcelled and the shopping bags shared out between us we make it back to the bus ahead of time. We sit watching the stragglers take their seats or stop and stand beside the partition talking to the driver. Then a wild-eyed woman with bright red hair arrives, and she keeps changing seats until she is sitting next to us. She smells of whiskey and clutches a poinsettia to her breast. Her eyes are wet.

"There was a little Mexican boy who cried all night because he had no present to give to the baby Jesus," she explains to my anxious younger brother. "But when he got up in the morning the leaves of the green hedge outside his front door had turned a beautiful red, just like flowers, and ever since the poinsettia has grown wild in Mexico."

Everyone makes a path for her between the shopping bags when she stumbles her slow way off the bus.

Clear skies beyond the lit bus windows. A promise of frost in the pastel dusk. Late crows on the wing. Cattle on the bare hillside, following a man with a load of fodder roped over his back.

We step off the bus into the dark and walk the road again, stopping at the stile where we left our wellington boots in the morning. Then take a short-cut through the fields, carting the shopping bags home. Lights in the house up ahead. Smell of hay on the cold air in the farmyard. And Daddy in his socks by the fire. A lamb chop stewing for himself in the kitchen. A pot of spuds freshly boiled for us, waiting for the mince and beans in our shopping bag for a quick dinner.

We burst into the quiet house and start tearing things out of bags. Even Mammy is in a rush to show Daddy the presents bought for relations and the children of her closest neighbours: toilet sets, children's bright woolly things, ankle-socks, face-cloths, story books, comics, tidy boxes of chocolates.

"They'll do grand," Daddy says, glossing over the presents. "Did you remember to bring cigarettes?"

We have our own parcels which are kept out of sight.
Stashed away in a bedroom for the time being. Nobody
leaves their presents under the tree in our house. We will
have the little gifts, the milk chocolates, pairs of socks,
paperbacks and ornaments we bought on the quiet today
ready to hand over on Christmas Day. As soon as we
have changed out of our good clothes we will separate
the gifts out on the quilt and search the house for clear
tape and a roving scissors to cut and make the wrapping
paper go round.

We are as restless as bluebottles after our day out, but
we do our level best to keep up this peaceful atmosphere
in the house by helping Mammy with the late dinner.
Daddy sits back in his armchair, the outside jobs done
for the night. We sit watching the television, our feet to
the fire, our presents put away until the big day, calm
again, the spending fever broken.

Daddy didn't have the right attitude to Christmas. He
seemed removed. Unconcerned. We were at an age
when we wanted all the details just right. Daddy was awkward. He ate slices from the Christmas cake well before
the holiday. He tore bottles out of the six-packs we had
bought in town, and he opened the visitors' whiskey before we had any visitors. And one year, when we were
old enough to notice he cut two pine branches, tied
them together with string and told us it was a Christmas
tree.

I took over the business of getting a Christmas tree
soon after that.

Off for holly first. Out the hill fields after the late
December rain lets up, the two dogs at my heels. The
ground soft, no colour in the short grass where hungry
pheasants have left their scrapings in the dead bracken.
A bow-saw blade over my shoulder, snug as a rifle strap.

Pressing through a hole in the hedge because I know a good holly tree two fields over on a neighbouring farm. The best berries grow right at the top, and I have to climb up through the thorn-protected and hard, green holly leaves to get them. Bite of the saw-blade on silver bark. White sawdust in the wind. A satisfying heavy red-berried weight in the fallen branch.

After the holly branch is carried home I face into a watery, winter evening sunset, the low sun punching a hole in the shower clouds. Reaching the mountain plantation at nightfall. The dogs whine to be lifted over the sheep-wire fencing around the plantation. Then I search the lines of trees in the dusk for a nicely rounded young conifer: prickly stem and the sharp pine smell of Norway spruce after the felling.

I wash my wellingtons when I get back and leave them outside on the street. Then I go up and down and all about the house until the green and red holly hangs in clusters over the pictures and the window frames of every room. Decorating with holly is an ancient ritual to safeguard the house and I know that care has to be taken to see that it is done right.

Out on to the front street again to stand the tree in a galvanized bucket with gravel and stones. Daddy going about the cow-sheds and calves' barns like any other winter's night. Bringing arm-loads of hay to leave at the cow-stakes; while I manhandle the tree into the front room, and then cut the wilder branches down to size using a hedge clippers. Last year's decorations in a cardboard box hauled out from under the bed. Baubles and spare bulbs for the fairy lights; a set of frosted glass bulbs which my mother said cost a lot at the time they were bought, but have worked every year since without fail once the loose bulbs are tightened in their sockets.

This is my favourite moment, a moment more precious

than the big day itself: sitting with the table-lamp off and only the flames from the open fire and the fairy lights on the tree to colour the room. The holly over the mirror, the carriage clock ticking and the dog asleep on the rug. Green forest resin smell in the room. A deep, satisfying finish to the ritual and ceremony of Christmas. The idea of peace and plenty in the world seems so real, so close at hand, drinking a cup of tea and eating from the tin of USA assorted biscuits.

On Christmas Eve the postman always stops for a drink in our kitchen. A clean-shaven, well-kept bachelor who lives with an unmarried brother and loves a chat with the housewives. He gets tea and home-made cake every time he calls with a letter – except when Mammy is out and Daddy is in charge of the house: then he gets bread and jam. He brings more Christmas cards on each of the closing days to Christmas, including Saturdays, in drifts of fresh white envelopes. The envelopes are done up in tight bundles for each townland, held together with fat elastic bands, and he is very careful and exact with the sorting, licking the top of his thumb as he goes through his post.

"A cup of tea, James?" my mother says as he sorts his letters.

"I'll have a drop in me hand, if you have the kettle on the boil."

Then he reaches deep into his canvas sack and brings out a card for my mother from America. It comes every year from her older sister: a specially bright card with a cheque made out in dollars in its folded middle. The postman smiles when he leaves the big card, with its air-mail markings on the envelope, on the top of the bunch on the sideboard. To have this one card for my mother makes him feel part of the house, included in the charmed circle of our family business.

My mother gives him tea, with the blue willow pattern cup set in its saucer, a slice of Christmas cake and a glass of neat, amber whiskey.

"Good health and a happy Christmas to you, ma'am," the postman says, his peaked cap balanced on his blue-uniformed knee.

It is his reward for bringing our letters and creamery cheques all year; for waiting in the kitchen with a cup of tea while my mother sits down to finish another letter for him to post; for taking messages and animal medicines between my mother and her sister who lives in the next townland; for telling us we have cattle out on the road; for letting us know that a removal is at seven, or a funeral on Friday morning after the eleven o'clock mass.

When he has finished his tea and whiskey he lilts a tune for us or strums a bar on the Jew's harp, killing another half-hour of his Christmas overtime. Then he walks up the lane, takes hold of his push-bike, his sack of letters over his shoulder, his oilskins tied and his parcels balanced on the carrier, and away he goes.

Christmas night and Daddy is gone to the pub, shuffled out of the way of mother and children. In the fellowship of all the other outcasts from the busy home kitchens of the valley he takes his Christmas drink in the front bar. Buying extra-generous rounds; spending a bit.

The darkness lies thick as a horse-blanket against the window-panes. But there is a bright light in the kitchen, where the Christmas cards hang on a string on the wall; Victorian gentlemen in black top-hats, winter singing robins and sprays of silver glitter, coach-and-four carriages and women wearing tied hats, bustles and ribbons. Snowflakes, candles and pine-cones.

We are Mammy's apron-string helpers, looking for small jobs to do and mixing bowls to lick. We help her to carry in the enormous, white, goose-pimpled turkey for stuffing. The kettle is breathing and the big pots left simmering on the black hob; plum puddings steaming in pudding cloths and double saucepans. Breadcrumbs tumble out of the metal grater to make stuffing for the bird. There is also a round of ham to be boiled, which will be roasted in the oven tomorrow with a glaze of brown sugar and cloves. We are a last-minute-with-everything family; one cake already half-eaten, Mammy has another Christmas cake to bake. She stands busy at the table with little cylinders of mixed spice, cinnamon, ginger and mixed peel. The raisins and sultanas are soaking in porter, and everybody gets a turn at the mixing bowl. Then we have blocks of almond marzipan to soften into a roll and fine icing sugar to wet and blend. My brother and I tussle in complete silence over who should be in charge of the little plastic figures used year-in and year-out, propped up in the icing to decorate the top of the cake.

If we have to go to the back door to throw tea-leaves in the hedge we can hear in the still yard the farm animals making tranquil animal gas sounds, chewing on their fodder as they lie down in the Bethlehem of our barns. Our mother has said it isn't safe to put candles in the windows all night – to light the holy family on their journey; too many fires have started that way. But every electric light in the house is left on, and standing at the back door we can see the hills full of lights, our whole townland and the distant countryside all lit up. Above our heads the stars are winking Christmas candles. Venus shines over the shoulder of the mountain like the guiding star in the East. The warm, spicy air from the kitchen is a premonition of wise Kings bringing strange and exotic gifts of gold, frankincense and myrrh. And the water in the winter drains tinkles like the jingle of bells announcing an old mystery.

The Christmas promise is even more intense when an older brother buttons up his coat to go to the midnight chapel. It is not that long ago since we would refuse to go to bed on Christmas night only we knew Santy was coming. We were past that now, but still close enough in years to be touched by the sensation of those Christmas nights when we lay awake and watched the steady moonlight at the end of the bed until we heard the men coming back from mass, talking and drinking soup in the kitchen. We had a plate of biscuits and a glass of orange juice left out for Santy. And at some hour of this magical night he would creep mysterious, and just a little frightening, into the room when we had tried for so long and failed to stay awake all night: just to hear the hoof-tap and harness-jingle of the flying reindeer on the ridge-tiles of our roof, or the rustle of soot in the chimney. It never happened, and Santy was never caught out. For years he filled us with a sense of never-to-be-matched anticipation. And we woke each year in a state of awe to find our wants at the foot of the bed on Christmas morning.

Over the years we found building blocks and jigsaw puzzles; paint boxes and colouring books. Dinky and Matchbox model cars with doors and bonnets that actually opened. Big bags of green plastic soldiers that were manfully posed with rifles and rocket-launchers, but were eventually left limbless and chewed to pieces – not by the machinery of war, but a new terrier pup. As we grew older and more ferocious there was a hullabaloo of cap-guns that devoured red paper rolls dotted with bumps of reeking gunpowder. Police badges and plastic handcuffs. FBI suction dart-guns and water pistols, and German Lugers that were black, detailed and deadly.

We were up with the sparrows on Christmas morning, and as soon as we had sorted through our presents we were off out the fields, half-dressed but strapped into our jewelled holsters, sheriff's badges, Winchester rifles and vinyl cowboy hats, with enough fire-power between us to rout King Kong out of the lower field.

No callers are wanted at the house on Christmas Day. We scrub and dress for first mass to be home early to start the dinner. The men on the road to mass are out with kettles, defrosting locks and tearing newspaper sheets off the white windshields of the cars. We take our seats in the perishing chapel and sit out a long sermon looking over at the crib in the chilly cross-house.

A Christmas morning fry-up as soon as we get home, and then we clean out the grate and leave the fire set in the front room. Soldiers' requests and second mass on the radio. Every man anxious to guarantee the smooth running of the day. The cattle turned out to the short hours of light, old bedding mucked out of the barns, fresh fodder left in. Logs chopped to work up an appetite for the dinner. Films and favourite programmes noted in the double-edition television guides and the fat Christmas supplement papers.

There are sprouts to be peeled and boiled. Plum pudding to warm in a bowl. Cream to be whipped for the topping to go on the trifle. And Daddy has to be talked into wearing his good suit after he has the outside jobs done.

"Don't be making such a fuss," he says.

But the real fuss is reserved for the turkey. Getting the heat up in the black-lead polished range and the roasting temperature steady – calculating the turkey weight against the number of hours in the oven. Too much heat and the meat will be dry; too little and the flesh inside the leg will stay pink. Everyone looks into the oven, opening the cooking foil wrapping to baste the bird in its juices.

There is a tussle over whose turn it is to make the brandy butter. And someone has to stand over the big cauldron of boiling potatoes to watch for the skins breaking open.

"Lift and drain them the minute they start laughing," my mother says to Daddy.

"There's not a smile out of them yet," he tells her, testing with a fork.

The extra leaf is opened out on the table, and by three o'clock we are ready to sit in, although we have to leave off watching in the middle of the early film.

"Is the turkey all right? I think the breast is a bit dry," Mammy says again as she serves up the dinner on the biggest plates we have in the house.

"No, it's grand. Stop fussing. The dinner is lovely."

It does not matter to us if the turkey meat is a little too pink or too dry. What is important is that range of familiar tastes of our traditional Christmas dinner: from the turkey breast or brown meat on the leg, to the brassy taste of Brussels sprouts, gravy and brown sauce. The brandy butter on the pudding, red jelly in the trifle. Tea and iced Christmas cake to finish.

Before long it is dark outside. The cattle are back in the barns, and everybody is stretched out in the front room, stuffed and over-full, talking over the television. Torn ends of wrapping paper and empty boxes are spread about the room after the swapping of presents; new jumpers and socks left aside. A box of milk chocolates is opened to relieve the deepening boredom and the sense of anticlimax. After all the effort and the anticipation Christmas Day is over and done with for another year.

"You won't find Christmas coming round again," Daddy says to tease us, and we all belly-groan in his direction.

Later in the evening we go to visit a schoolfriend's house to take a hand in a family game of cards. Games of twenty-five for small coins, with best fireside-chair fathers who have a knack of dealing all the good cards to themselves and turning up their own trumps.

"I have a crow's nest," these canny fathers complain as they raise the pot of matchsticks and pennies, and peer down their nose at a winning Jack of diamonds, a five or an ace of hearts. Familiar, predictable, reassuring. Then the turkey carcass is stripped for sandwiches.

On Stephen's Day we dress up as as wren-boys and go the rounds of the roads. The sad, skeletal remains of a near dead tradition. We make our masked arrival in baggy coats and old clothes out of parcels. Thinly disguised, with perished hands holding a tin whistle or a flageolet, we are only in it for the pennies, collected in a jam-jar with a slot cut in the lid. The sleet gusts about a windy front street. We shake our pennies in the porch. A dog barks inside the farmhouse door.

"Mammy, Mammy, it's the ramble boys," an excited child shouts from inside.

We start into a short, tuneless version of "Silent Night". It is a relief to everybody when we take the money and immediately move on.

New Year's night. Lace of snow on the ground. Daddy out on the front street with the shotgun. Shots fired into the air. More guncracks echoing about the valley at the stroke of midnight – frightening the witches out of the bushes around the house.

First thing in the morning on New Year's Day I put a

new calendar on the nail, and then I have visits to make in the falling wet snowflakes. Visits to houses where it is still thought unlucky to have a red-headed stranger for a first caller. I am brought into council row cottages and two-storey farmhouses alike, to have tea and biscuits, lemonade and shiny shillings pressed into my hand for my dark hair to bring a share of luck into the house. Like the holly over the door, the fairy lights on the pine tree, the shots fired on the street, another magic charm to secure the home, to protect and hold the family together.

There is a cock-step in the days after Little Christmas; a thaw on the slush roads walking to school again. The family box of milk chocolates is long eaten and New Year resolutions melt away like the snowmen with coal-nuts for eyes in the front gardens.

It was back in these schoolrooms and playground that the rumours had started, that doubts about Santy came my way. Suspicions were cast on flying reindeer and letters posted to the North Pole.

"There's no such thing as Santy."

"Yes, there is."

"No, there isn't."

"Prove it."

And the clues and hints coming up to Christmas led me, after a top-to-bottom search of the house, to the wardrobe in Mammy and Daddy's room. Standing on a chair to look in over the top where the toys lay waiting. My heart might have cracked open at the sight.

I was discovering a world where presents were ordered with a down payment weeks in advance, left aside in the shops, and finally hidden in the house by Daddy – often on the very day we went off shopping on the bus. Daddy had been to a different town while we were out. Our presents were put out of reach until Christmas night, when he crept into our room in his socks and left the presents on the dressing table or at the foot of the bed.

I began to understand something about my parents then; how they worked their own magic to hold the house together. The care and trouble they took to meet our needs, to see that we felt secure, loved.

Every year the promise of Christmas was met. Our needs were discovered early and letters to Santy kept by the postman. A fresh turkey was bought for the table, and on shopping trips into town ends were made to meet. Keeping up appearances until we were old enough to understand. But if there was the pain of losing Santy there was the comfort of finding a different Father Christmas. A man who worked hard to provide for us, but hid his feelings as successfully as Santy could hide our toys until we were asleep.

When it was all out in the open I had to promise not to spoil the Christmas magic for the younger ones. That sense of permanence and security, of family love and gifts conjured out of nowhere. It was my first big adult secret: keeping that Christmas promise.

Out With It

A THREE-ROOMED SCHOOLHOUSE AT the top end of the valley. Low walls around the playground built above the river embankment. Curve of shallow, stony river below the school gable. Rough-cast walls and the blue Bangor slate roof shining after an April hailstone shower. Sunlight on the long glass panes of the timber windows that slide down from the top on lead-weighted sashes. An open to the weather front, and the varnish peeling off the long plank bench seat in the perishing lunch shelter: girls' toilets at the upper end, reeking rough cement boys' toilets at the bottom end. Seagulls and scavenger crows in the playground waiting for bread crusts.

Kate Ann in brogues and a home-sewn pinafore, up in front of the teacher for talking out of turn. Gruff voice and farm ways: better at bucket-feeding a small calf with two fingers dipped in the warm milk, holding down the head of the wet-nosed suck-calf snuffling up its drink, than she is at keeping her nibs safe, or the blue ink smudges out of her copy book.

Departures

Miss Gunning, standing by the pot-bellied stove where the teacher's pet bottles of tea are kept warm. Her glasses shining and her lips sucked tight together. No words spoken amongst the onlookers: pale high-infant faces to the blackboard in their usual state of silent terror. Sitting still in the hinged double seats, ink-well-fitted and pencil-grooved oak desks. Older girls reciting their nine-times tables for the headmaster in the next room.

Using a sally rod – cut from a roadside hedge with care – as a pointing stick Miss Gunning directs Kate Ann to hold out her hand. Silence. Then the air whistles with the speed of the first slap. A small, red-welted hand drops and the stick signals for the second hand to be raised for punishment. A fast-stinging stroke, and through the swish and cut of the air Kate Ann says:

"Aisy, ya bitch ya."

Oh, the Pain of It

I'M SITTING IN THE HISTORY class in a hard plastic chair, listening to the details of some campaign or uprising unfold, knowing in my heart that long before the lesson finishes a traitor will appear and the day end in tears. It strikes me that there are certain parallels between the sorry course of our native history and my own schooldays. A shared history of bruised ideals and constant rebellion against a standing authority.

After every forty-minute class period we are shunted between the shabby, overcrowded rooms of the main building across the asphalt and rain-pooled yard, and a shanty town of weathered wooden prefabs, erected on concrete blocks around the County Vocational Education Committee Technical School, know locally as the Tech. Seven subjects on our daily curriculum, we circulate in a clockwork movement along the foot-tracked corridors smelling of damp duffel coats, egg and onion sandwiches and wet feet in canvas sneakers. Jostled among ill-fitting jumpers and outgrown trousers with windy gaps at the ankles. Pimple-worried, the dandruff showering about our bottle shoulders, the hair standing on the backs of our heads, noses wiped on the backs of hands, and all mouths open, taking in air through the hard, sweet-rotted remains of our milk teeth. Glib among the first-year girls, stomach-punching rough with each other, dragging about ball-and-chain heavy schoolbags of hand-me-down standard textbooks. Miserable to a man.

Down the corridor Mr Boland lopes among the latecomers and ducks with a Monday pink face past the principal's office. A textbook under his arm rolled tight as a military baton, he enters into the reek of science-room chemicals.

The commotion dies away as we take up lines along the wipe-down, Bunsen burner valve- and sink-fitted benches, toying with the hope of a butane gas explosion. Mr Boland sits by his large, raised desk, litmus paper dry in the mouth, among report stands, tripods and test-tubes, incubating his hangover.

"Higgins."

"Yes, sir."

"Report."

"Yes, sir."

"Parts of the digestive system."

"Moran."

"Yes, sir."

"Report."

"Yes, sir."

"Peristalsis."

"Prick," says a disgruntled voice from the back.

Tommy "the trout" Higgins is brought up to the blackboard to sketch and label a diagram of the pancreas, stomach and duodenum, done in coloured chalk. Every drawing is taken straight out of the Folens textbook, traced on to the blackboard, copied into the graph paper side of our science exercise books, and then safely forgotten. We sit there writing all day, longing for practical experiments with dangerous chemical salts and battery acids, boiling liquids, hydrogen explosions in lidded gas jars and disgraceful operations on frogs.

"Quiet down the back," Mr Boland shouts, and we start into our scribbling again.

Mr Boland is both science teacher and amateur boxing coach, and when he has an eye to sport he rings us in the lower end of the room for the hard lads and braggarts to spar and jab and scuffle. After school Mr Boland motors his shadow-boxing and iron-jawed Mohammed Alis in an overloaded yellow Austin to county boxing club matches. The Mountain Mauler versus Scrap Iron. With Scrap Iron, our school bully, landing back black-eyed and sullen after a first round trouncing. And Mr Boland barking at him:

"Join the art class, McGinley, if you're that fond of the canvas."

Autumn has the fresh ink and glossy paper smell of new schoolbooks. Our seasonal return to the classroom is regulated by the headmaster's new, complicated and unworkable timetables in early September – withdrawn, photocopied and written over each evening as the long-term teachers vie for power, and fob off early Monday and late Friday evening classes on dogsbody part-timers, PE, art and civics teachers. But all too soon our course is steadied and corrected. The results of the summer examinations come back from the department and we are divided into ambitious A classes, where all the brainy girls go, and rebellious B classes – dead-end dumping grounds for bed-wetters and the wilfully dumb, the daft, the depressed and the disturbed.

With our fate fixed for the whole long treadmill year we are welcomed back by the headmaster, who gives us a pep talk on the wealth, health and status our further education will bring us in the end.

"Keep your noses to the grindstone, boys. A good education is easily carried," he says, as he stands before us in his horn-rims, age-old gabardine trousers, thermal vest and ravelled cardigan.

Then off we go to our various rooms to meet his muttering and frequently mutinous staff, each wearing the same thin union ties and the same drip-dry terylene suits, with ends of chewing gum stuck to their backsides.

The first day back in the sawdust, bench-marked and every tool in its place woodwork room Tommy Higgins opens his finger with a chisel. In the solder-, flux- and oil-smelling metalwork room each man raids the next locker down the line to make up a full kit of tools – metal punch, hammer, file and square. Owen Keegan, the last man in the line, is found locked inside the store-room. In the mechanical-drawing class Tommy Higgins makes two halves of his T-square, and there is not a single man with the right grade of lead in his pencil.

It's the same story every year. The same fixed syllabus year in and year out, as predictable as the block letter writing and lovehearts inscribed on the desks. Even our dodges stay the same. Going for a seat at the back of the class and being brought up to the front with the regular miscreants. Forging notes from home to go down town at lunch-hour. Taking nosebleeds, sick stomachs and fainting fits. Togging out and begging leave for football practice in the middle of the mechanical-drawing class. Smoking in the toilets, loitering in the corridors, wandering about half the day looking for a chair. And every other remaining free minute is spent with our coats buttoned up tight, sitting on the storage heaters.

Witness, too, the same poor scholars every year who come in early to cog the homework. Sitting at the back of a quiet room every morning to hurry answers before the bell goes for the first class. Hearing the echo calls and young commotion from the volley-ball court, and the howling protests when the ball is deliberately dropped in a silted puddle and bounced off the back of a man's head.

The horseplay, the headbutts and the bullying order of each school year. A head pushed down a toilet or held under a running tap in the sink. Threats of teeth shoved down a throat. Fist-fights under the sheltering wall of the basketball court, ending with a grazed knuckle, a black eye, a jacket torn. More scores waiting to be settled. The nicknames, the breaking voices and the broken windows of every school year.

It has become second nature to avoid the staff-room windows where the tea-drinking teachers delay over their pennywise biscuits, bought from their weekly kitty, with a cake on Fridays. They sit and talk about union dues and limited liability. Savage insight is the weapon we use against their authority. And when the class bell rings and they come out of their corner we take them on in turns.

Mrs Caulfield, eighty or more: snow-white head, yellow nerve tablets and a constant cigarette, mauling us through our mathematics. Twisting our ears to haul unwilling brains over Pythagoras's theorem, which she calls the bridge of asses.

"The ... the square of the hippopotamus ..." Owen Keegan stutters.

"*Amadán!*" she roars in his face.

A living terror to us all, and not a sign of her retiring. Square rooted in simultaneous equations and the binomial theorem to the last of her days.

Miss Trivet, the house-coated domestic science teacher. Needlepoint sore and taken with a pinch of salt.

Mr Kennedy, dry as a blackboard, smirking geography.

"Tuam," he says, and cuts off an inattentive nose at the back with his flying chalk.

"Produces shoes, grass and molasses, sir," you say. Every county you could name in those days had a bacon factory and a tannery: shoes, grass and molasses were always a safe guess. The rest of the time you just sit there pretending you don't exist.

You know that Kennedy has moved to the back of the room and is standing somewhere behind you, but you dare not turn your head. You sit as still as a stone in a field, hardly daring to breathe, only to find two heavy hands pressing down on your shoulders as your memory of provincial towns, longest rivers and the average rainfall in the midlands dwindles to a trickle.

We are glued to the television set every spare minute we get, watching live transmissions of the Apollo moonshot. And Miss Hartigan, the Irish teacher, gives us Peig Sayers to read – a record of the hardships and misfortunes suffered by a barefoot drudge from the Blasket Islands, whose only comfort in life is following coffins to the graveyard.

Father Logan is a short, stout, frog-faced man with a heavy topcoat, shiny shoes and a warm, unchristian car on rainy evenings. His religion class is compulsory, bringing out a familiar sort of know-it-all, glib malice in everybody.

"Father, if God is all-powerful could he build a fence so high he couldn't jump over it?"

"Could he make a rock so big he couldn't lift it?"

Mostly, we just fold our arms and glare as he passes out Good News Catechism books with awful pen-and-ink drawings of Christ and the Apostles, in which someone has drawn a cartoon Jesus who rises into orbit as you flick the pages past your thumb. And written into a balloon over the drawing of this Ascension are the words: "Gentlemen, we have lift-off."

And then there is Mr Connolly, the English teacher, pulling on his chin and pursing his lips over a longed-for cool pint come four o'clock. The taste of porter mulling amongst Manley Hopkins and Charles Dickens. Essaying to the pub on pay evenings. After a lifetime week of listening to long-faced lads of fourteen, already able dealers at the cattle mart, and girls only waiting to baby their laps, rhyme off Shakespeare in a nasal monotone to the rhythm of their two-times tables. He turns his back to the class to list adverbs and pronouns on the blackboard, while yawning students have their lunches stolen, their flasks broken and their bags smuggled out the window. Doing the rounds at lunch-hour he finds someone's school-annotated edition of Jane Austen floating in the urinal.

We may riot and boast, lark with the girls and speculate about the time of their periods, write slogans with felt-tip markers on the seats when we get to the back of the forty-five-seater yellow school bus, but we are silenced by the arrival of "Blakey", the school bus inspector, waiting out the road in a Renault 4 car to spot-check our regulation green school transport tickets. We arrive home humiliated, dog-tired and brain-dead from school, our evenings a misery of homework. And school reports saying: "could do better"; under which I write: "could do worse".

Night brings the oppression of an always hot kitchen. Five years of it in all. From a noisy inaugural first day throwing paper gliders about the room, to the last high summer day of sweating leaving certificate examinations. A dulling of the senses and a low-pressure mental depression that tasted of packet soup-thickened stews, mashed turnips, stewed apple and custard.

Back in the school yard we cluster in blood-brother-close gangs of twos and threes. Reliable school pals holding off trouble and mockery, going over the unsolved problems from the night before.

"What answer did you get for question twenty-three, part four?"

"Thirty-three point three-three."

"I got one thousand and eight."

"Did you get the French done?"

"No. Madame Duchamp's plates are still *sur la table* since last night."

Rainy lunch-breaks are passed together playing table-tennis. Good days are for hard-fought games of handball against a high gable, or pitch-and-toss with copper coins aimed tight to a spud stone. In between we follow the league table standing of soccer teams across the water, better than any periodic table of the elements. Outside the four walls of school we can't be bothered looking at a map of the country, but we litter the bedroom walls with posters of our soccer heroes: Charlie George, Gordon Banks, George Best, Bobby and Jack Charlton. Kick football out in the fields with friends until the dusk hides our jacket goalposts.

And then to be called out of a cosy, stirabout warm bed on a rainy Monday morning to meet the school bus. Envious of the dog curled and safe in a wet day nest of old jumpers. Wishing it would freeze and leave the roads like a bottle and the bus wouldn't make it. Thinking of hiding a school bag in the hedge and spending the day mitching down town, playing truant under bridges or roving out among orchards. But usually obediently waiting at the crossroads, sick to the bottom of my boots at the thought of all that unfinished business in my brown paper-covered exercise books and another savage day in school.

There are longed-for half-days and closures due to snow. And there are those strange scholars who are absent all year but arrive in on the one day the rest of the school is off with a seasonal flu. The same scholars who turn up in class whenever it snows: battling their way in through the blizzard to take a seat at the front when all the teachers and regular pupils are hoping that class numbers will not rise above a handful and the headmaster will have to call the bus drivers to say the school is closing early.

For a breath of freedom in these early blue-line copybook and leaky biro days we idle about in gangs on bicycles, speeding down the hills and skidding up the gravel in front of the girls.

I am cheeky in a full company, and tongue-tied when left alone with the one girl I fancy. Lovesickness comes with spots. And the quick sense of teenage shame is primed to burn on my face in deep, frequent and unpredictable blushes. But my arm is eventually tested around a girl's shoulder sitting around a summer holiday bonfire. There are longer kisses shared walking home from a dance. Exchanges of rings, neck-chains and T-shirts. Followed by a busy trade in love notes. The hand-medown rituals of first love.

Back in our national school-going days visiting magicians and touring animal shows stopped outside the school yard on an open lorry; with scrofulous rabbits, one-eyed bantam cocks, gerbils that might have been shrunken rats and sad, wet-eyed hamsters. And there was a day each year when we dipped our plastic combs under the tap, cat-licked and dressed for the school photographer. In the Tech we have the school tour, which means a day-trip to the Spring Show.

I tried and failed to save money for the school tour each year in a battered post office savings book, but it came down in the end to the powers at home to say if I was allowed to go; to pay the bus or train fare, to press pocket-money into my fist on the way out the front door that morning.

Waiting for the school bus had a different flavour that day. My senses were wide open for a change. Open to the smell of cobweb-misted hedgerows and damp disturbed gravel on the way to the crossroads. A sense of excitement as physical as that smell of waiting coach diesel smoke and padded seats. Together with the mingled perfumes of shampoo and toilet soap after a good scrubbing behind the ears. The rub of a new collar around my neck.

The brave girls wore scent. The teachers wore dry-cleaned suits retired from the classroom the year before. Everybody took a different head-count looking down the bus as we set out for the Spring Show. Up the road the driver sat waiting for Miss Trivet, who always got the job of rounding up the strays that went missing at every stop.

"Higgins, you'll be late for your own funeral. Why is it that you can never be on time for anything?"

"I don't know, Miss."

It was a day when you dared to swap banter with your teachers. You were still among schoolfriends but away from the slog and cram and punishment of the classroom. This was your chance to navigate your own course about the capital city. To stand dauntless with a brown tray in the queue for an egg, sausage and chips dinner on a first encounter with a self-service restaurant. To wink with the big boys smuggling cider and cans of shandy on to the bus. To cheer on young outlaws smoking first cigarettes. A practical science lesson on the effects of mixing strong tobacco and alcohol, that soon resulted in pale faces changing to traffic-light green, and ended with someone throwing up in a paper bag without a bottom. And you could easily guess which way the pre-vailing wind was blowing when Mr Boland and Mr Connolly went off for a pub lunch; leaving Miss Trivet to finish the junior tour around the agricultural machinery spare parts, the hoof-rot sprays, the new brands of worm-dose and sheep-wire. We had wised up enough over the years to drop out of these useful information tours and educational stands to shop for our own catchpenny gim-micks, Kiss Me Quick hats, pocket-knives, farting cush-ions and itching powder – the boys from the B class bought water pistols.

I grew closer to the back seat each school tour year. Year by year, outside the official curriculum, I had learned how to trade love tokens and French kisses. To find my own use for the English language: sending February Valentine cards and waiting for love letters with the coded initials I.T.A.L.Y. and S.W.A.L.K. printed along the edges of the sealed envelopes. I was still serv-ing my apprenticeship of lovesick and sleepless nights under the blankets with a new transistor, listening to Kid Jensen on Fabulous 208, Radio Luxembourg. I knew that I would always be shy about sharing sweetheart seats until the very end of the day. There were smirking boys who would always hold fast to their water pistols, but there was a rare comfort which was not to be missed in that company of low, quiet heads leaning together under shared cardigans or coats. Oh, the pain of it. And the re-lease from pain. Squeezing an ounce of love out of these adolescent years on that night-returning bus.

The summer holidays slip away. The nights are soon taken up with homework again, half-done between bouts of pain-killing television. Back again for another long year in the classroom. We had been offered a glimpse of the larger world on that annual school tour to the capital. The world we are supposed to conquer if we knuckle down this term, put our trust in the headmaster's new timetable and the power of the free education system. The teachers keep repeating that the time has come to forget about the soccer and go for a real goal: a job in the bank.

New Islands

THE DRUIDS FELT IT WAS on the edge of water that poetry was revealed to them. And I associate rivers and river-banks with the dawn of solitary wanderings.

From the gable window of an upstairs bedroom of our house on the mountain I could always see the serpent bends of the river, on its horseshoe journey around the valley. A black river under grey Atlantic skies, a silver river in summer sunlight, a pure blue river in spring, a brown river in swollen winter flood.

The valley took its name from the river – Arigna, the destroyer. It grew as the rain fell all day and into the early dark and low-cloud evening. A downpour through the night, drumming a sleepy tattoo on the slate roof. Eave-runs spilling into skillet pots and rain-barrels. Moving pebbles that set a pulse in the streams of water on either side of the road. Water pooling against the ditchbacks, and the washed-away lanes.

And it was still raining when we got up to bring in the brow-beaten cattle standing under the dripping shelter of ivy bush and hawthorn. Smooth, wet pelts on big-muscled thighs sucking at the muck in the gaps, making slow progress to the barns. The cow-tracks full of water. The slippery pasture sponge-wet and flooded in the hollows. More rain at the back of the mountain.

You could feel the brooding, elemental force of the hills, where the line of fields met the rock and the grey, wheeling cloud. The rain pressed down heather clumps, bog-cotton, scutch grass and bilberry stems. The fresh streams met on the bog lanes, dislodged stones in the black peat, cutting deeper ruts in the turf; flooded into the old channels and hooped briar culverts. The white-water rumble swelled in the ledged slate and hazelwood alths; foaming, peat-tinted torrents tumbled in the gully.

From the mountain plantations, far up the valley, the brown flood came, rising quick and breaking the river-banks, eddying quicksilver in the low fields. The outlines of the river flattened and spread out.

Swift, mud-foamed water carried bottles and rags, and plastic shopping bags. Floating big, white-weathered limbs of trees lodged at the piers of the red iron pipe and concrete footbridge we called the balk.

Men with land at the river moved anxious cattle to high ground. My grandfather with his feet warming on the hob said: "I wonder if these boots are waterproof?"

"It's fireproof boots you'd need, Tom," my father answered.

The gable window opened for a better view of the river grown twice its size. And there was an urge, then, to be out there. To task the elements. My brother and I, wool caps, anoracks, hot faces and smelly wellingtons, headed down the fields to witness the mud and wash of the evening, wading through waist-high rushes, jeans darkly drenched to our thighs. A yelping terrier chased nimble rabbits exiled from the wet earth. We went down to the moving borders of the flood, to outwit the torrent, to busybody and survey, defying the flood to rise beyond our young courage.

We grew impatient with the river and the never-to-let-up rain when we knew it was just another flash flood and not a Pacific tidal wave wreaking historic destruction. And then we would have to plod home in squelching boots to face our mother after another wetting.

Waiting for the flood to go down you could always head for the mountain, taking the bog lane up to the big rocks, the foxhole crevices, the back-tracking hares, and the man-keepers in the bogholes. To see if the sweat-houses were still standing; if the lintel stones of the abandoned homesteads had fallen; if the thatched turf-stacks sheltering verminous bumble bees had taken in water. To see if the monument stones, heather stretches, turf-banks, sphagnum moss and nesting grouse, old quarry face and closed mine shafts were still in their places. The air washed clean between the hills, the squint of shining lakes, the nimbus smoke over village chimneys and the map of roads of the several counties spread under the lip of the hill.

Then there was a blue opening in the eye of heaven, and with the flood gone down we walked the river-bank to see what the torrents had dislodged, carried down or carried off, to see what new face the copper-brown flood had minted on our river islands.

We would cross through the fields and the crouching holes in the hedges, taking the drains in one jump. Penetrating fairy-tale deep blackthorn patches to see the badgers' straw beds drying in the mouths of their dug-outs and setts. Clambering up the embankment to the railroad – a narrow-gauge line run into the ground be-

fore our time. Rusting notices on gates, old bolts in the
cinder-bed, the level track a sloe-hedged home to the foxglove and birchwood. The seasoned sleepers standing in
the gaps like checkpoints at the farm borders.

We knew the locations of all the bridges hidden under
the grass-grown railway. Some that were low and dark,
and were a test of nerves. You bowed your head and en-
tered a low, dark mouth and watched iron-red water rise
towards the rims of your wellington boots, feeling the
weight and pressure of elver-quick cold water press the
rubber against your legs, waiting for a cold spill into your
boot if you stumbled in the deep, and the darker places,
where spider-webs tickled your face and black millepedes
coiled in the stonework and imagined bats hung above
your head, waiting to get caught in your hair.

We measured the subtle changes in the shape of our
river islands and deltas, gathered the animal-bone drift-
wood, and looked for marbled round stones, egg-shell
brittle clay pipe stems. Biscuit-brown and honey-cap
glazed jars with curling handles, coloured bits of crock-
ery, old remedy bottles with names printed in the glass,
car batteries, animal skulls, paper-fine fish spines and
punctured footballs. Keepsakes.

We would get together at the river-bank for gang meetings and the building of stepping stone bridges and rick-
ety rafts, which we launched at the shallow fording
places. We listened to the plunge and suck of the water
as we dropped big round rocks into the deepest turnholes; fished with fat worms hooked out of jam-jars;
spent hours skipping flat stones across the water. Then
we floated bottles on the current and hunted them down
with stones in fierce competition; lobbed stones ranging
outside or inside the bobbing prize; followed along the
bank until the target was broken and sunk. The vandal
instinct appeased.

Later, balancing a pair of borrowed black binoculars on the middle bar of the gable window, I brought the brown and green plantation-belted bulk of the opposite mountain into focus in a rainbow-edged prism. A mountain standing a whole heart-lifting day away.

Or, lowering the line of sight, I followed the path of the river, with its virgin banks of yellow gorse on either side, to the place where the river mouth met the lake lying miles off in summer haze. It stretched over three miles, from Corry strand at one end of the lake to the roaring sluice gates of Ballintra at the other – where a reluctant ass would only walk the timbered bridge above the roaring floodgates with a hemp sack pulled down over its stubborn head. Big timber gates, iron cog-wheels and pulleys, falling water and concrete fish-passes for the leaping salmon, the brown trout and the shoaling bream.

We knew stories of an island down the lake where skulls were kept in the gaps in the stone walls. And of how a woman visitor had made off with a skull to be used as a novelty sugar bowl: until a red blood stain spread through the white sugar granules in the upturned skull. From that same place old men told of a flagstone that floated out on the water to collect the dead and ferry them over to their island burial place.

At the end of the lake, safely above the roar and pull of the sluice gates at Ballintra, lay O'Connor's island; a tangled woody place offering the challenge of new territory.

When the sun had bleached the rainclouds fleecy white and the leaves stood crisp against the blue sky, we went speeding down the mountain on bicycles. Morning shadows on the gables and the trees flashing. Dog daisies and dandelions and sweet-grass in the margins. Then over the humpback bridge spanning the rock-cluttered, sandy shallows of the native river. Cleg-pestered cattle standing knee-deep in the water.

We followed the fishermen's paths down the last part of the river to the lake. Studied the grass-capped and cut-away ledges; the dangers of edging too close to the eel-dark turnholes drummed into our heads. A couple of pike fishermen's boats lay tied up at the mouth of the river, the wooded mystery of O'Connor's island up ahead.

We came out on sun-warm, black sand-flats. The lake far out, the level gone down with the opening of the sluice gates, releasing power to the downriver generating stations. The leaning fence-posts cut from alder and willow were visible again; risen from the lake, fishbaits and green nylon lines hang on the rusty barbed-wire.

We navitaged the bridge of land that welded the island to the shore in summer, rolling up trouser legs to wade the sharp-cold and gleaming shallows. Pressed through the undergrowth to an empty royal house at the centre of the island where we found a monkey-puzzle tree and disturbed water-rats the size of otters. Later, we sat and watched a gawky grey heron standing amongst the bul-rushes, saw the long-necked cormorants dive for min-nows, and glimpsed a perfect blue kingfisher spearing the lake. We pressed and labelled marsh marigolds be-tween sheets of paper. Our journeys outward were get-ting longer, the natural mysteries mingling with the words of our schoolbooks.

Ten years on and I was still going down to view the river habitat in its different conditions, arriving at the river-bank and sitting under the green alders. The river had cut new tracks and courses, shifted and silted fresh deltas, found new islands. White rags from high-water floods hung in the branches, torn edges touching the black water. Mirror edge on the water by the weir. An oracle calm. A place to surrender to the energies that spring from within the new-made mind. The first lines of poetry forming on the tongue.

Bus Connections

SHOALING OUT OF DUBLIN WITH the early Friday
evening crowd. Over O'Connell Bridge in a head-
bobbing current of pedestrians, past bootleg tape
and pavement jewellery sellers. Leaping out into the
stream of oncoming cars and green, leaning double-deck-
ers at the intersections. Tangled in the waiting lines at
the bus-stops, and watchful for the reckless weaving of
helmet-hidden, hot leather, oil- and rubber-burning motorbike couriers, with walkie-talkies and satchels strapped
to their backs. A weekend migration from sea-smelling
Dublin city streets towards small lake-front farms, rebel-
held stone bridges and brown-river country towns. The
young offspring of thirty-acre holdings. The sons and
daughters of proud, blue bank-book and deposit account
holding shopkeepers, rural sergeants and dry-stock farmers. Away for a week in the city on a first wage after the
years of hard-paid-for and home-supported third level education. Heads banded with personal stereos and coat
pockets bulging with paperback books, magazines, mineral cans and Mars bars. Hungry for home-cooking, and

carting travel bags full of dirty laundry for the kitchen washing machine.

The cockleshell-roofed Bus Éireann terminal, a lofty wind-tunnel in winter, is a sea of bags and backpacks. A coat-over-suitcase crowd, queuing for tickets or roving about the park-bench seating. Black diesel smoke rising from the rear ends of coaches reversing towards the numbered doors. The jostling and anxious queues tighten ranks, well-mannered and -reared, but not wanting to miss out on a seat home.

In Connolly station the Belfast train is delayed. The queue for the north-west-bound Sligo train stretches all the way back to the slatted escalator that is forever out of order or blocked with hard-headed gurriers sliding down the handrails. And no matter how far you walk along the platform, or what carriage you choose, you finish sitting opposite a dandruffed priest suffering from indigestion after his morning fry-up over the *Irish Independent* in the dining car. Or a big country woman with a hand-knit cardigan escorting a little nun home on holidays. Waiting in the next carriage is a hand-shaking and talkative drunk, or a sullen and wordless teenager dressed in death-worship black and Doc Martins with a concentration camp haircut.

Further on out the road the hitchers are posted along the inside lane, from the Spa Hotel at Lucan to the pillars of the pedestrian bridge at Maynooth College and Seminary. Waistcoats, packet tobacco and roll-your-own heads with cowboy hats, leaky guitar cases and lanky girlfriends. Waiting for lifts, with cardboard signs reading: "Galway Please".

Some get lifts from past martyrs of the road, promoted from torn desert boots to Renault 4 vans, re-sprayed but still walking with rust. A sunflower-yellow and smiling "Nuclear Power No Thanks" sticker in the window; in the back, baby things and shopping bags, bulging with celery, natural yogurt and kiwi fruit.

But most will be lifted by angry, fat, tie-strangled men, heavy smoking with hardened arteries and coronary pink in the face from too many whiskeys gulped back in the travellers' watering-hole hotels. Men who are angry at the state of the country and the weather, angry at big business loans and ministers' pensions, pop music and teenage morals, layabout students, medical-card holders and consultants, Oxford diets and the price of antacids. The radio out of tune, the car too hot, the windows fogged and the seats full of dockets, they storm and thunder for miles over a landscape of private insults, scandals and grudges.

The long-serving fleets of private coaches, bottle-necked at Enfield, roll through Kilcock at the rate of one a minute, steering round by the canal bridge where the next generation of bored, after-school teenagers dangle their legs above the dark water. The coach routes fork down the road in Kinnegad, turning for Galway, Athlone and Tullamore, or going straight on to Sligo, Cavan town and Donegal.

Passengers sit high above the passing road, reaching up and directing air-vents that wheeze a stale breath of warm air in summer and send down icy gales in winter. They test the switches of small circular lights, watched by a driver who knows that he alone controls the power to illuminate the jumping print of rolled magazines, early evening papers and Maeve Binchy novels. And the radio brokenly tuned to 2FM.

Strangers without Walkmans pressed into opposite seats and general conversations.

"How many is in the house with you?"

"Five lads and me."

"I'd say the frying pan sees a fair bit of action."

On through the familiar midland towns: Mullingar, Longford, Carrick-on-Shannon, branching for Castlerea and Strokestown, Tubbercurry and Westport. Marking off the miles with familiar shops and pubs and petrol stations in the falling dusk. Dropped down with your bags in a wet town of just one main street, a fire station and a housing estate. Rain falling past the street-lamps and the lit windows of late evening grocery shops. Then a solitary car with a trailer hitched to the back passes through on its way from the dump.

You arrive home to the welcome of a family dog, the gardening programme on the television, supper, the *Late Late Show* and a film as old as the hills before closedown.

The normality of it all after the chained bicycles, the narrow bedsits with the awful wallpaper, the mince too often for dinner. The spaghetti and sausages, the toenail clippings in the carpet, the tiny portable TV with wobbling reception and no licence. The unionised and unfriendly pub lounges run like factories. The peeping-child-filled Chinese take-aways. The tiny tomato sauce containers and damp salt sachets in the back of the press where you put the rent. Tom Waits and Mary Coughlan tapes. The lonely evenings in dressing-gowns.

Country girls sharing rooms together, still several years short of a secure suburban lifestyle. Girls too new to the life to feel safe: still nervous of the city streets by night. Girls who go very few places all week: early to bed weeknights, and up steady for work in the morning, in the flatlands of Malahide, Ranelagh and Rathmines. Hiding out in rented properties owned by double-mortgaged guards. Staying quiet in the cramped and burgled flats and rooms of the North and South Circular roads. Living in anticipation of these home weekends. Civil servants and front counter bank staff, part-time schoolteachers and engineers, trainee managers and trustworty

accountants, nurses doing courses in midwifery, tidy sec-
retaries and distracted receptionists, graduates just out
of college, with the flat accents and honest looks
favoured at city interviews. The pimpled boys and sensible blouse with pleated tartan skirt for work girls who
staff the city for Dubliners.

Friday nights are for chores waiting since last week, for
watching the television in comfort, or a late trip to the
local for a pint and a game of pool with friends returned
to the neighbourhood for the weekend. On Friday nights
you are home again from the pub in time to meet a
mother waiting up in her dressing-gown.

Sunday is the papers and a family afternoon roast of
lamb or chicken dinner. And then off in squashed cars to
a county football match.

But Saturday nights are for hometown discos. The lads
have planned their strategy, rated the venues for pints
and women.

"Did you get off with Martina Donlon last week?"

"I didn't get within an ass's roar ..."

The women have swapped comparisons for the *craic*,
music and men.

"Susan and John have broken up."

"Are you going out with anyone yourself?"

"Sort of ..."

Endlessly discussing the chat-ups and the let-downs of
these big Saturday nights out.

Nine o'clock and the men are heading out fresh-shaved
and dabbing pin-spotted bleeding chins with toilet tissue.
The taste of toothpaste on the tongue before the first
pint. Strolling in leather jackets and bright trousers, trail-
ing bargain-basement aftershave, fingertips brushing a
rough-cast wall on the way down the street, condoms in
the wallet, thinking this will be the night.

The women are already circled about the pub table; in high heels and white trousers, or the short black skirt and a cigarette.

The mini-bus loads of Saturday night regulars leave early for the nightclubs from the three-man band in the corner lounges, the Karaoke shouting matches, the brewery T-shirt and a ticket with every pint promotions. From ten o'clock to closing time the buses ferry boisterous and combat-ready passengers from the town pubs to the discos built out the road, a world of low-roofed nightclubs out the country – from Ballybofey to Mohill, from Ballina to Corofin.

Barn-size hotel extensions with spinning coloured spotlights, mirror-balls and epileptic strobe lighting. Cigarette smoke sticky plastic ferns and chrome pipe stools, see-through tables and stale carpets. A small square of wooden dance-floor. The late extension bar counter taking up a whole long side wall.

There are coloured ribbons tied to the wipers of the cars in the carpark – the late remains of a Saturday wedding. Early arrivals for the disco meet the wedding party left-overs in the front bar. Tired air in the hotel after a long day that started with a roll of narrow red carpet in the hallway. Leading to the sherry reception and the wedding breakfast, served at long trestle tables with paper tablecloths and turkey and ham dinners dished out by a sullen army of part-timers. Big helpings at the kitchen door end, cold gravy at the other end. The women in rival outfits and shoulder-pads, holding down their hats in the breeze. The wedding party delayed by the photographer. Tall men with big hands and loose ties down pints before the dinner. Speeches, telegrams, and the brandy-jolly father of the bride making jokes saying, "Many's the time we ate out of the one egg."

By ten o'clock the tables and the wedding guests have

been cleared away, and the nightclub doors are opening to the public. Low vibrating music throbs through the colour-splashed high window-panes.

"Fix bayonets," says the man in the front of the queue.

Pay your money in at the hatch and take a supper ticket. Search the already airless dark as you enter, go to the bar for drink and then join the usual roustabouts ringing the regular table loaded with pint glasses and heaped empties waiting to be shattered with brave war-cries and cheers.

"We might not go to mass on Sunday," shout the wide-boys impressing women, "but we drink religiously on a Saturday night."

If it's not a disc jockey jabbing the dizzying light buttons and play switches and shouting out birthday requests, it's a live band on stage, doing cover versions of the current chart hits. A hopeful female singer fronting a bored bass player and a curly, long-in-the-tooth guitarist. She is either short, raven dark with tranquilliser lips, or leggy with big cleavage and a platinum mop. She is aped at all night by brave pint-glass-clutching welders and panel-beaters shouting, "There's no rust on that body."

"Like the old diesel twenty tractor, I'd say she'd still flatten a few meadows."

It is an old testing ground, and strength comes from the most outrageous remark. Ever since you were first smuggled in by an older brother or sister to a disco there has been this familiar business of buying drink, sharing cigarettes, the manouverings for attention, the scrapes, the escapes, the knowing squints, the testing touch of the arm or shoulder. And the prepared put-down to prove you don't really care.

"Go on, ask her to dance."

"Are you joking? She has a mouth on her like a half-door."

"What about her friend?"

"She looks like a cat stuck up in a tree."

Gusting laughter prevails in the lee of jokes memorised from comedy video tapes and alternative TV. There are night-long slagging matches with comings and goings from the table every so often to try a dancing partner. Nodding at unheard words over the music during the fast numbers, separating in the wait for the slow sets. With trips to the toilet to save face.

But some have said all the right things, made all the right moves and found that loving or just willing other; out of view of the milling dancers and drinkers they take to dim corners, blind to the world and its scruples.

The music hammers, the heat rises, the drink cushions. The shifting glitter of the spotlights could be sunlight playing over water. The dancers wriggle about like minnows in a brimming jam-jar. Predators shadow the borders of the packed crowd. There is the makings of a brawl to be avoided at the top end of the bar, and a scrum of drunken men, arms linked, lurching heedless and falling through the dancing couples. A smell of farts on the dance-floor.

The steel shutters are coming down on the last orders and you have to bend and strain over sweaty shirt-backs bull-roaring over the counter for drink. Shouting thanks to a familiar barman when you get served: "You're a horse of a man, and a pony tail to prove it!"

Come the end of the night and the man with the car-keys is missing.

Quiet drivers and shy mineral drinkers, who have stood alone all night, find a crush of vaguely known men and now so friendly women around them looking for a way home. The bar-staff wipe down table tops and herd the late drinkers towards the exit doors. The bouncers lift the chrome stools back on to the padded seats, and steal away forgotten full pints off the tables to be drunk in a back room. The boys from the back of the mountain spit in the drinks they can't finish.

The drunks stagger footless out of the hot cinders of the smoke and lager and brimming ash-tray night.

"Where would you be without a bell on your bike and your shirt wringing," shout the veterans of the long walk home in the summer ground-fog.

Newly matched or seasoned couples leave together. Gaggles of girls are organising cars. Independent women with their own transport round up stray passengers gone off to sluice the dark back gables after beer.

The white trouser girls are dumping once eager and now abusive partners. Kisses, frustrations, arguments and partings. Clothes smelling of cigarettes and spilt beer, breaths sour, collars ringed, make-up spoiled, out-fits drink-stained, heat-sullied and crumpled. Dulled salmon after the spawning.

Out into the cool, dark pools of star-dotted night and off with the lurching drivers, mindful of the checkpoints and the breathalyser tests, taking the back roads home. Passing out cigarettes in packed and grateful, tight-shoul-der crushes in the back seats of home-bound cars. More car-loads going back into town to the chipper, hungry for greasy but sobering cheeseburgers, onion rings and cur-ried chips. Six-packs shared out amongst the diehards, for one final fling before the sun rises on a sore-lunged, hungover and hounded out to mass Sunday morning.

Another weekend ending with no special conclusion. Just a lift to the nearest Sunday evening station or pri-vate coach stop. You set down a sports bag full of folded shirts and clean underwear at your feet as you pay the driver and board the late bus back to Dublin. Rented house keys jingle in your pocket, your nostrils anticipat-ing that chilly, unlived-in air as the door swings open on an empty flat. You dump your bag on the bed, pour an out-of-date carton of milk down the sink and stock the cupboard from a plastic shopping bag with some things you've bought for the morning.

On the Market

IT IS A WICKEDLY COLD, windy Tuesday in January. The skies are leaden, the streets bleak and cruel. The windows and doors of the small town are tightly closed. No shop will open before ten; and then, only for the odd smoker, gasping for a cigarette and eager for the headlines and obituaries of the morning paper. A tractor rolls through town and a cow bellows into the dreaming bedrooms, to announce the first mart of the New Year.

The cattle mart is a low building tucked away behind the town in the solemn shelter of the church and graveyard. The wind cuts over the bare remains of the old fair green, whistling through the corrugated-iron roof and empty cattle pens. Lorries, tractors and vans appear out of the grim morning, rumbling across the gravel forecourt. Small men sink deeper into big overcoats and tighten down well-worn caps as the wind whips along the first, sharp pellets of hail. Drivers climb down from lorry cabs:

"Hardy weather."

"You wouldn't put a ladder out this morning."

After a cold start on the bare hill-farms the farmers in Volkswagen Beetles begin to appear. Crawling down the street, hunched and half-awake and hanging out of the steering wheel, they squint and scowl at the day ahead.

The morning advances, and a thin winter light slants over rooftops pebbled with hailstones. Smoking chimneys show signs of life. Street doors open to reluctant dogs and schoolchildren rubbing eyes crusted with sleep. The pavements echo with the footsteps of sniffling scholars, bent with the cold and a burden of satchels.

The tractors and trucks form a ragged line in the mart yard by the unloading chute. Tail-gates come down and the animals rush blindly into a narrow cattle-crush to join an ordered single file, their brute strength contained by unyielding steel bars. A lock of hair is clipped from each broad back, a gob of paste goes on and a sticker with a number is slapped in place. The drovers collect cattle identity cards as you enter: export certificates a welcome bonus.

I surrender my animal, my card and export cert and make a note of my number for when the selling time comes around. The big-eyed cattle are herded along in the pens, bewildered by capture. All around, prized animals and proud owners are being separated. It is difficult to tell the animals apart now, as they are swallowed up amongst a score of similar shorthorns, black-pollys, Friesians, Limousins, Charolais and all the host of breeds in between.

In trots a mangy redhead. A poor cow, reared on rushes and louse powder; all skin and bones, a shabby coat, a long face and a broken heel. She is sent to the isolation pen for the day. Forlorn, forgotten and jeered at by better-fed farmers.

"Where did they find her?"

"Down from the far mountain, I'll gamble."

"Where the snipes wear wellingtons."

Inside, only one sales ring is in use today. Even the cattle seem subdued. At a busy mart, when you first plunge into the hot, reeking air, the uproar can be deafening. From a tubular steel maze of cattle pens and crushes packed with bellowing animals the steam rises from beefy flanks, wet snouts and the slippery, unwholesome floor. There are sudden roars from the booming bottoms of big-lunged bullocks that rattle the corrugated-iron roof and loosen the teeth in the mouths of old and yawning farmers.

Through the hot, sticky air, full of the smell of cattle and commerce and tobacco smoke, move the brown-coated cattle drovers and traders. And mixed amongst them are the shifty buyers, dealers and jobbers, asking devious questions and getting devious answers. And nobody giving anything away.

"What did you get for the heifer you sold before Christmas?"

"Ah! I got nothing for her. What did you get for yours?"

"I got half-nothing."

The men shout orders and discuss the prices and are here to do business. There is one face that appears every mart day. A man with the tops of his wellington boots turned down, his greatcoat tied about the middle with a hand-spun rope of hay. Ready for a day spent clambering over crowded cattle pens; tugging furry lugs, pinching the flesh of well-fed heifers, hankering after a slap along beefy haunches, that means more to him than a holiday by the sea.

"You wouldn't meet a finer animal in a day's walk," he declares, pulling at a wicked bullock's tail, delighting in the antics of maddened animals.

The business at the loading pens wears on long after

midday. Then the crowd begins to gather around the sales ring. Over all the noise and steam and smoke comes the voice of the auctioneer. The real business of the day is about to begin. In a tight circle with a sawdust floor, the animals do a reluctant turn for the buyers. A bucking black-white-head gets a smart smack of the stick and shows a none-too-clean pair of heels on its trot around the ring. A haughty Continental Charolais, with garlic and molasses on its breath, does a lazy circle for the buyers and then lifts its tail before leaving the ring, unimpressed.

The buyers hang on the side of the ring like drowning men clinging to edge of a raft. Shoulder to shoulder and cool as poker players they scrutinise every animal. Their trade is a miracle of co-ordination: eyes fixed on the chosen animal, ears tuned to make sense of the machine-gun rattle of the auctioneer. Their hands waving and signalling prices and bids with pointed fingers, open fists, raised eyebrows and a Masonic handshake for good measure. Orchestrated bids coming from the pit to the auctioneer conducting business from the podium. To be a good buyer you need an eye for a fine animal, a nose for a bargain, a thirst for a killing and a sixth sense no school or university can teach.

Above the ring on the wooden steps, big enough to double as bench seats and made to measure for the long strides of mountainy men, stand tight rows of sturdy and critical onlookers. With a dangling Sweet Afton, a bent pipe or the smouldering butt-end of a Woodbine gummed to a lower lip, this grim-faced jury watch the weights and prices. The business of the day is chewed over and, this being the New Year, often with the resolute sucking of a mint.

It would be fine to be a spectator today, but I have an animal to sell. I stand above the ring waiting for any animal that might pass for my own. Then I listen close to the bidding, measuring the selling price against my expectations. The neighbours at my back mutter oaths and sigh their discontent, chewing down the ends of their blackthorn sticks waiting for the outcome. When it is all done they pronounce that it was an unfair contest. The buyers had it all their own way. The seller was robbed.

"It's a disgrace. I don't know what sort of job you'd need to keep a farm going today."

I nod and fix a price in my head and swear I'll not sell for less.

After a long day standing around the ring the cold and the hunger creep in; through felt hats and flat caps, through mufflers and duffel coats, flannel shirts, long-Johns, and trousers the size of collapsed tents; through jackets burst at the shoulders, patched at the elbows but torn again at the sleeves; through greatcoats tied with string and anoraks with the quilted stuffing hanging out, the cold comes creeping deep into the brittle marrow-bones and frozen hearts of bachelors without breakfasts.

It is time to retreat to the mart canteen. To the clatter of plates, the ring of forks and scraping knives. To the bubbling of hot soup and jolly women. To a steamy, hot, stew-smelling atmosphere where motherly women serve plates heaped with marbled and tender beef, mountains of mashed potato, crusty brown or white bread, with butter, buns and a portion of swiss roll.

Sitting about the formica-topped tables men stiff and silent with the cold rub calloused hands before wrapping them around scalding hot mugs of tea, or settling down to the tastiest, most welcome dinner of the week. In such a place a woman can lead a hungry miser into temptation.

"Go on, be a devil, and have some desert as well," the busty blonde teases, bending close to a willing ear.

A broken man, he fingers a rusty clasp, pokes and searches his old leather purse, and surrenders his savings to this sweet-talking Eve, offering a bite of sinfully sweet, hot and spicy apple tart.

Back at the sales ring it is time for me to take up position amongst the tense and anxious faces beside the auctioneer. My number comes a little closer with every turn of his slate. Each time he dusts off a number and chalks up a new weight in kilos, my day advances by another digit to that critical moment when I will have to sell.

It has been a long day since we first loaded the animals, clattering and scraping up the slippery tailboard of the truck under a hail of oaths and threats from a length of black plastic piping. Several hours have dragged by since I followed the slow procession of tractor trailers into town.

With time to kill I have walked past the trucks selling young calves in the depths of fodder-rationed and hungry January. Past vans with the back doors open displaying oilskins and donkey jackets, wellington boots and worm-doses, paraffin lamps, spades and spraying machines, rat-traps and candlesticks. The last reminders of the old street fairs.

The days of the horse trading between farmers, the spitting and the hand-slapping, the luck-money and the practised intervention of onlookers are gone. The dealers want only well-fed and finished animals. The order of the day is for lean beef for Continental tables. Casual banter remains but the talk hinges on the latest round of EC levies, subsidies, supplements and penalties. The only thing that counts now is that big clock-face above the mart ring that speaks in kilos. The common language of the Common Market.

The town trade slumped when the street fairs died. In

the mart no money changes hands and deals will finish a week later with a cheque in the post.

In the old days wads of money were exchanged. And the farmers' wives came into town. A posse of head-scarfed women riding in on a rivet-rattling rural bus with a chesty diesel engine. They brandished long shopping lists; raiding drapers for woollen blankets and candy-striped flannelette sheets. They demanded winter duffel coats and sensible shoes for school-going children. It was a day for settling bills, buying treats and bringing home chirping boxes of day-old chickens. And the straw and leatherette shopping bags bulged towards bursting again. With the dealing done and the cattle tethered on the green the men crowded the bars and butcher shops, and never left town without a parcel of meat.

It is all so impersonal today. On a small farm like ours the animals are as well-known as the children. Though the cattle are there to make money the woman of the house has petted and coaxed them along since they were small calves. She has bucket-fed and suckled them with her fingers. She has weaned and foddered them with hand-picked best armfuls of hay. She has cleaned their barns and made their beds with dry straw. In the evenings she has walked the fields to bring her strays home before night. She has nursed them through runny noses, sore eyes, scours and coughs, talked to them.

"Suck ... suck ... suck. Poor little fella. Is your drink too hot? There's a good boy. I've picked a nice bit of hay for you. You'll eat that, won't you? Now, don't turn up your nose at me."

She has yelled at them, cursed and forgiven them: for tramping her clothes off the line, for breaking into her garden and eating the early cabbage plants, or biting the tops off spring flowers. She has fussed over buckets and tested the temperature of their milk as often as three times a day. She has plugged draughty holes in dry-stone barns and blocked up windows with rags and hay on the severest winter nights. She has wrapped the youngest and weakest, most spindle-legged new calves in blankets of wool when pneumonia threatened, and reared them until they were strong, thriving cattle running home with a dog at their heels.

My number is next on the slate. I hurry to the walled-off space behind the auctioneer where an animal that has been worried over for so long will be disposed of in a matter of minutes. The ordeal begins the moment the animal troops across the weighbridge and the long arm of the clock reaches after those precious extra kilos.

"What am I bid now for this fine animal? Who'll start the bidding at four hundred? Three fifty? Three hundred? Don't insult the man. Who'll give me three hundred?"

The auctioneer goes on demanding money and I stare at the floor until the starting price is settled.

It is a foreign language spoken by bidders and auctioneers all over the world: frenzied and distorted through ancient, dusty loudspeakers and rusty-voiced microphones. Meaningless to some, it is music to my ears. A melody of rising prices, of ever-increasing bids and still holding out for more. My body is rigid with tension, but I have seen connoisseurs of the cattle bidding trade lean grandly across these same hard cement steps, as comfortable as any Cleopatra on a feather divan.

"Keep her going, keep her going," says the voice inside my head.

The auctioneer turns and calls over his shoulder: "Do you want to keep us here all day?"

I shout back: "No sale."

Finally, after coaxing blood, sweat and tears from the

stoney-hearted buyers, after a dozen exasperated looks from the long-suffering auctioneer, after stubborn silences and pleas for one last bid, after all life seems finished around the ring, I give the nod.

"On the market."

The tongue-trotting is over and it is a final gallop to the finishing price. My animal is transformed: the flat-footed bullock of the morning becomes a Grand National favourite with my last penny riding on his back. In the final seconds the visions of all that hard work, all the effort to get this far, cloud the brain. The auctioneer's voice means nothing now. It might as well be a loose lid rattling on a boiling saucepan or a small dog furiously chewing butterscotch.

The bidders are exhausted at the last. It is a slow-motion finish as the auctioneer coaxes one final effort. There is a loud crack, as sharp and final as the fall of a guillotine blade, and the gavel comes down.

"Sold."

The auctioneer turns to me and says:

"It's a legacy you're getting at that price."

I step down, exhausted. Beneath the big coat I'm as limp as the auctioneer's thin paper docket in my hand with the sale price written in black and white. I got a good price and perhaps, but only perhaps, the others at home will be happy and not tell me I should have held out for more.

Outside, the dealers are loading their purchase. They will slip out of town the back way as soon as they finish in the mart office, on their night drive back to the docks and factories. I take a short-cut across the old fair green. The town is quiet again: a shop girl mopping floors, a barman chatting to a customer, and dusk falling on the old fair green.

Return Ticket

FOR THREE HOURS WE HAD been just one small particle in the endless stream of traffic, all new cars on a flawless road surface high on concrete pillars. Looking down on islands of rural life between the motorways. Looking down on neat, brown-brick farmhouses and barns screened by trees. Surveying through car passenger windows the regular flat fields of maize, potatoes, glasshouses, lettuce and beans in flower. Every available acre of ground had been utilised to the full and laid out in a grid of canals, and everywhere there were poplars in elegant straight lines evenly spaced along the waterways, where still reflections gave a greater symmetry to this lowland scenery. Nothing out of place in a landscape where wealth equalled order and order equalled beauty; where human beings appeared to be just small parts of a bigger machine. We left the motorway and followed the blue signs into the town centre. And the silver lines of cars in the sun were metal corpuscles, the motorways veins feeding into the heart of the beast.

In the evening I went out walking through the Dutch

town in an open-neck shirt with the sleeves rolled up. Warm, continental air. Crowds of people everywhere, wearing blue denim like a uniform – manicured, tanned, healthy, affluent. European. Not a freckled nor a snot-nosed child with a soft cough in sight.

In the town square a fleet of trucks were sweeping, scrubbing and polishing the cobblestones after a free open-air concert. The musicians were still packing up when the cleaning trucks arrived.

I stopped for a beer at a pavement table outside the Vilderman bar. It was close to midnight, but I sat outside under the wall-mounted North Sea gas heaters and drank cold Heineken beer from a tiny glass through a high collar of foam. Then I sat back in my chair and listened. The people were friendly but I didn't speak the language and I had to make do with the native guttural sounds and the gestures of disdain, trying to nod my head at the right moments to appear included.

My attention kept turning back to this one girl sitting at the next table. She was sitting with a thin young man who wore a beard and kept his ankles tightly wrapped around the leg of his chair. Her eyes had guessed my interest.

"You're English," the girl said, when we both ordered another round of drinks, and then sat waiting for the busy white-aproned barman to return. "I heard you speak."

"Irish," I said. "From the country."

"I was born in Devon," the girl said.

"A beautiful place, by all accounts."

"Yes," she said. "But I was packed off to school in London when I was very young. When I finished there I moved to Amsterdam."

I glanced at the young man, but he was looking at his hands.

"I work in a shop, selling chocolates," she said. "The Dutch eat a lot of chocolate."

"Do you speak the langauge?"

"I'm quite fluent by now, but I have an accent. People are always asking me where I come from."

"How long have you lived in this part of Holland?"

"About two and a half years. I didn't like Amsterdam. Too many weirdos there. I travelled around for a while and then moved here to the south. This is the real Netherlands."

"So you've gone native."

"I couldn't go back to Devon now," she said, and fell silent.

"The next thing you have to do is marry a rich Dutchman," I said, searching for something to say.

She tilted back in her chair to look at the young man. "We're getting married in three weeks' time," she said.

The young man nodded his head. "Only I am not rich," he said, slowly, uncertain of his English.

"You don't have to be rich to marry me," the girl said.

"This is a rich man's country," the young man said.

The barman arrived with the drinks and started to leave down fresh beermats on the table. The girl opened her handbag and took out a bright twenty guilder note.

"I'll get this," she said.

The young man looked at me. "You see? I am a Dutchman, only I have no money."

"I don't care," the girl said. "You'll find a job. I'm not marrying you for money."

We raised our drinks together and touched glasses.

The girl turned to me. "It's the voices I miss. I'm never homesick, really."

London was my first stop. I thought I knew the place from watching so many hours of multi-channel televison.

But I felt estranged, conscious of my standing; walking in a city blessed with bookshops and galleries, but also crowded with the grey and ponderous monuments of Empire.

"Pat," the Cockneys said in their cheery way, and the nickname rankled.

Sun-mirror glare from the office windows. The city of business. Mannered. Impersonal. High-rise. I had never seen so many Rolls Royce cars with tinted windows, or so many millons of people moving underground, noses pressed to page three nipples for privacy, flashing wordless through the tube stations.

I stayed on emigrant friends' floors. Living out of the zip pockets of a rucksack and a nylon sleeping bag. Bringing in take-aways and carry-outs. Counting funds that were meant for longer journeys. Searching the travel office windows for cheap destinations. My romantic grand tour: Amsterdam, Provence or the Pyrenees. Paris or Barcelona. Fulfilling that need to get away from home. To escape the parish pump outlook. Leaving the known territory to join that summer migration of young tulip-pickers in Holland, grape-pickers in France, factory workers in Germany, hotel staff in Guernsey. There were times when I felt like a stranger in London. Attitudes were different, but the currency was so nearly the same. London was a compromise between at home and abroad. A way-side station before the Continent.

I stroll on a sunlit Sunday morning along the leaning streets of Montmartre in the city of Paris. The air is fresh, the streets clean; invisible sparrows echo about the eaves and the damp, walled gardens. The rattle of a corrugated iron van delivering new-baked French bread, *baguettes* as abundant as matchsticks in the delivery man's arms. A gendarme wearing a pistol. A black congregation walking to chapel. And a thin-shinned whore with a scarlet mouth making an early start in a doorway on the opposite side of the street.

"On the crest of a wave, or thereabouts," as craggy Samuel Beckett would have it.

Passing a wordless afternoon wandering around the cobbled and narrow district of the Marais. All Renault cars parked under shuttered windows and flowering nasturtiums in the window-boxes. Francs and centimes in my pocket. Boules tossed in the fine dust of the Place des Vosges at the fall of evening. An orange moon above the park. Voices in the dusk of a foreign city.

Night brings me back to the dry vineyard hills of Montmartre, to view the black velvet-lined bowl of the city jewelled with light. Around the Place du Tertre the young masters of the freshly daubed chalk and charcoal, dabbed and oil-dappled, original but done to a formula paintings for the tourists, are packing away their paintboxes and easels. The sketches still in progress of ballerinas and side-street scenes taken down until tomorrow. The caricaturists and silhouette cutters pocket their paper and scissors. Above it all, the white, floodlit stone of the basilica of the Sacre Cœur stands remote from the crowds. Serene. Separate from its surroundings and the hawkers everywhere – poor, back-street opportunists and shabby immigrants getting by in an adopted city by selling over-priced junk; mechanical birds, luminous jewellery, leather belts and hats that smell like dog-pelt. A different gimmick every season, fishing warm coke and beer from plastic buckets for the late night visitors.

I walk for miles every day, carrying a folding Métro map and a romantic history of this city in my head. For company I imagine Hemingway quietly drinking Rum St James in a good café on the Place St Michel; James Joyce browsing through his proofs in the back of Sylvia Beach's original Shakespeare and Company on the rue de l'Odéon. Scott Fitzgerald escaping the small-town Prohibition mentality of America on the boulevards of Montparnasse in the 1920s. Utrillo at his easel painting the intimate meeting of these small Parisian streets. Or mad Gérard de Nerval, walking a lobster on the end of a blue ribbon in the Luxembourg gardens.

"I have a liking for lobsters," he said. "They are peaceful, serious creatures, and they don't bark."

I call on the graves of Oscar Wilde and Jim Morrison in Père Lachaise, in a state of silent curiosity and devotion. At the zinc counter of a poky little *tabac* in the old quarter I buy a beer and stamps and picture postcards of the domes of the Sacre Cœur rising over the rooftops, garrets, shutters and iron-balconied windows of the pale sandstone dwelling houses on the Quai Anatole France. Then I dream of the poet Arthur Rimbaud, a lonesome figure searching the garbage pails and sleeping under the eyes of the bridges; sketching the solitary illuminations of his youth.

I am a looker-in-windows, a price-tag and menu reader. A mute witness cut off behind a crystal-clear obstacle of language and inside addresses. I watch with an outsider's disdain the mollycoddled, air-conditioned coach parties disembark and congregate about the dusty steps of Notre Dame, or mill, foxed and dog-eared, about the booksellers' stalls along the quays. But I journey with them up the narrow stairs of the cathedral to visit the rabbit-eating and pensive carved stone gargoyles. I want to take complete possession of this city, standing on the heights with my map open, placing the landmarks along the *café au lait*-coloured Seine.

Days abroad go by, and with the exception of the closely guarded grass of the formal city parks, Paris seems made for a walking penny-counter, as I carry my passport and an essential big bottle of mineral water in a canvas knapsack over my shoulder. Walking spares me the ordeals and hot-faced humiliations of negotiating even simple business in new denominations and in another language for which I have no talent. And walking always eases that nagging worry of ending up utterly broke and by myself in a foreign city; keeps my mind from counting my remaining money two times over.

Saturday evening comes warm and close. I feel some unnameable ache or longing. The little side-streets echo with the bustle of weekend shoppers as I step out of my cheap hotel on the rue Notre Dame de Lorette, where I have a room at the back offering a view of cast-iron drainpipes, brick walls and kitchen refuse bins. And I, in turn, have left my socks soaking in the sink. I enter the rue des Martyrs: a shopping street with these by now less alien French names over the traders' doors – *boulangerie, fromagerie, boucherie* and *pâtisserie*. High art, even in the window displays. There are canvas-hooded street stalls selling shellfish, shoes, exotic clothing; and unbelievably narrow supermarkets where ordinary Parisians shop.

I sit down to eat in a restaurant I've come to know, even if I am not yet known there by name. Pressed in elbow-close at the table. "*Bon appétit*," exchanged with a bulging woman in a short black dress sitting opposite, engrossed in a plate of pasta. I hand-signal and gesture for nothing extravagant with wine.

It is shortly after midnight as I enter Pigalle. Tourists throng the sidewalks. The pungent aroma of sex hugs the air, smothered in the diesel fumes of the coach tour buses lining the street. The new Moulin Rouge is doing good business at a price beyond me. I enter deep into the aroma of Greek sandwiches, hot-dogs and beer froth on the zinc bar-tops, and yes there are garlic dressing and Gauloise fumes, and native Frenchmen who indicate

their wealth by the depth of the reek of their cigars and
their eau-de-Cologne.

I make my way past the whores whispering out of the
shadows; past the peep-show and hostess bars. A pretty
girl on a high stool near the door and wearing no underwear offers an eye-opener for any man. At the hotel desk
the black doorman is watching an old episode of *Star
Trek*, dubbed into French. Back in my hot room I pick
up nothing more exotic than a book, and spend the
night reading about a Paris peopled with rag-pickers,
painters' models and boulevardiers:

> *Whenever people talk of pleasure, of clandestine love, of
> ephemeral liasons, ruined eldest sons ... one's imagination
> turns irresistibly towards Notre Dame de Lorette.*

Lying there on my pillow roll I am filled with a sensation of quiet joy. This romance with a foreign city is
enough for me; a romance without dialogue. Just being
here; seeing and surviving.

Then the money is gone. The last few francs are spent
on a bus to the ferry port. But the minute I look over the
rail at the dock lights falling back, and the harbour
mouth opening before me, the voice of the open road
whispers in my ear that I was just beginning to fit in. It
was a mistake to carry a return ticket.

Trying to grasp what it means to be back again in the
Republic of Ireland. Back to the familiar voice of Gay
Byrne's radio show in the mornings. The Angelus bell at
noon and another eighteen-bell call to prayer at six in
the evening. Back to a new breed of churches without
steeples, pastoral letters on contraception, and Labour
party church-gate collections. Big fry-ups for breakfast.
Flowery Kerr's Pinks for the dinner. The poverty trap
and the National Development Plan. The main roads
only widened in patches on European Community grant

money. Speculators digging up the beauty spots, the environmentalists fretting, and the planners getting it wrong. Back to dole days and District Courts, Income Tax and influenza, potholes and loose Aran Banner mouths. Back to the grey clouds left on the ground, endless soft shawls of rain and lonesome Sunday evening towns. The damp agri-tourism guesthouses and the rod licence dispute. Open skies, rugged pasture, unruly hedgerows and small-acre farmland running to wilderness. Country roads with a flood on the inside of every turn. The jerry-rigged, littered and makeshift. But the comfort of hot whiskey in the snug on hard nights. High barstool arguments leading nowhere; quick, off-the-cuff remarks – the good ones – that say it all. Sitting on for the after-hours drinking and then hiding from an unarmed constabulary shining flashlights in the windows of dim, speakeasy, crossroads pubs. Old boys looking for a lift home with a grab of the elbow and, "I'll be up the road with you."

I look on at it all with a traveller's critical eye. A starved priest of the road, thumbing a lift on the last leg of the journey home. The fat driver's belly shakes when he laughs after he asks, "Are you coming from the football match?" and I answer, "No, I'm coming from France."

I have returned to a very un-Irish heatwave. Temperatures are creeping into the eighties in the fine mercury line of the thermometer. The tar is boiling up at the crossroads, the streets spattered with milky ice-cream spills. Dogs panting in the doorways. And there is a general election underway.

Extravagant posters of the party leaders wallpaper the town. The lesser party members have their mugshots tacked to pieces of two-by-one laths along the roadside telephone wires, in keeping with an old Celtic preference for worshipping tribal heads on poles.

On the hall floor there is a wedge of campaign leaflets and hand-bills in free-post government envelopes, and letters with photocopied signatures asking for a personal vote. Men in suits riding the campaign ticket to power, shaking hands and walking the housing estates on the television news. I'm seeing it all at one remove: if only these people could see what these eyes have seen the issues would be different.

I am back, but I still feel like I'm outside all this; standing on the sidelines. And the sensation is just as strong as it was in London, the Netherlands or when I first arrived in Paris. Nothing engages my interest, nothing roots me here until the first canvasser calls at my door. I ignore the ring of the doorbell and then catch him looking in the front window. A big man in a tight suit huffing in the unreasonable heat.

"I'm very weak," he says, when I open the door to tackle him.

"Sorry?"

"I said I'm very weak."

"Do you want a glass of water?" I ask. "Maybe you want to sit down for a minute?"

"No, no. I'm canvassing, do you see. I want your number one."

"My number one?"

"Aye, that's right. Your number one. I'm very weak."

"But who are you canvassing for?"

"Meself."

"Can you tell me what party you're from?"

"I'm from the mental hospital."

"I see. They know you're out canvassing, I suppose?"

"They threw me out. They want to close the hospital. I'm canvassing to keep it open."

"Why?"

"I want to get back in again."

A Small Rebellion

"WE'LL DAB," DADDY WOULD SAY, whenever it was time to leave. Now he is gone.

It was the end of October and he had come down with a cold. We had visits from the lady doctor. The fire was revved up in the kitchen to warm the room for an examination. My father dressed and came down from the bedroom and sat close to the hob. We listened for the car outside. I met the doctor on the front street and escorted her into the house. Then my mother closed the panel door and waited about doing small jobs in the scullery, or just outside on the back street. The doctor was patient and kind to him. We all knew it was dangerous.

After a discreet absence my mother came back into the kitchen to set a tray with tea and biscuits for the doctor. She found the two of them talking and smoking together. Out at the car, when the doctor had isssued a prescription and was giving me a few tablets in a bottle for my father to be going on with she said:

"You could try keeping him off the cigarettes, but it

would add nothing to his life now. He won't change and you couldn't hope to give him more than a month. The withdrawal symptoms and the suffering involved would make his last days a misery for everybody, especially for your father."

I suppose he had been smoking since he was twelve or fourteen years old. Sweet Afton, with the Robert Burns poem printed on the box:

Flow gently, Sweet Afton, among thy green braes,
Flow gently, I'll sing thee a song in thy praise.

Or war-time Woodbines, sold singly or in the original blue packets. As a boy it was daring and forbidden to smoke while watching Hopalong Cassidy in the picture house, and as a young man in the fifties it was fashionable and without danger, even for all-action cowboys and matinee idols. Later, in the public bar, a pint wouldn't be the same without a cigarette. But there was a history of weak chests and asthma in the family: brothers and sisters had died young. But he loved his cigarettes. Couldn't do without them.

"Would you ever run down to the shop for ten cigarettes and a box of matches," he'd say, just when we were all settled for the night, watching the television.

Then the song and dance would start.

"Could you not wait until the morning?" my mother would say. "Give your lungs a rest. Can't you see the cigarettes are killing you?"

"I'll go myself," he'd say, going out into the hall and putting an arm into his coat.

"No, I'll go," I'd volunteer, knowing that if he went he would spend the rest of the evening in the pub.

He wasn't a late-night drinker, more a four o'clock until eight o'clock man. A bunty-tailed terrier followed him everywhere he went and always sat under his seat by the window in the front bar. He would meet the pitmen stopping off from work, and drink with them until the crowd started to come in. The young bloods called him "Scampeen". Part mockery and part affection. The talk ranged from cut cats to pruning roses to the proper way to eat cream crackers with a priest's housekeeper over a good carpet.

Then he would ask one of the lads to leave him up the road. He would buy a round, and when they had finished their drink they would drop him at the road gate. He took his time on the lane. Stopping to bend in the middle, leaning his hands on his legs just above the knees, waiting to get his wind back. You could hear him coughing long into the dusk. The terrier would grow restless and leave him then, rushing ahead to meet my mother in the yard, where she was getting the last of her jobs done in the failing light. She knew my father took blackouts when the colour of his face turned deep red and the coughing bouts deepened to a noiseless spasm. She couldn't sit easy in the house until she heard him coughing in the lane and she knew he was back again safe.

He wasn't long in the door before he went upstairs to bed, the clock radio turned up. When supper was ready my mother would call up to him:

"Are you coming down for a cup of tea."

"Bring it up."

"Bad luck to you, couldn't you do all that for a person?"

No anwer. Just the sound of the radio.

"Do you want a bit of currant bread with it?"

"Aye."

The battle was to get him to cut back on the Woodbines, and then to get him to change over to filter-tipped cigarettes. In the beginning he would just break off the filters and smoke the remainder down to a damp end burning on his bottom lip, his jaws two stubborn hollows sucking the last drag of smoke out of the butt. An American aunt posted on a set of six brown plastic filters of different lengths and strengths that were designed to lower his need for nicotine in stages. He used one of the shortest and weakest filters for a week or so, and then only when we were watching. After seven days of neglect in the bottom of his pocket, amongst the small coins and loose tobacco, it was in such a foul state we had to accept defeat. The battle had been lost a long time before, but in the last months it was hard to take it when he started up his Ventolin nebuliser, a clear plastic mask over his nose and mouth, breathing in his medication in a compressed air spray to open the pores of his lungs. And the minute his lungs were ready to take in the oxygen he lit up another cigarette.

"I know the cigarettes are killing me," he'd say.

"It's psychiatric care you need," was all my mother could say in return.

He spent hours up in his bedroom reading short articles out of *Ireland's Own* magazine and listening to the clock radio. Sitting up in bed at the mention of the corncrakes in "Pat Murphy's Meadows" in summers long ago. And he was very fond of Tommy O'Brien: an unlikely radio star who specialised in playing the opera greats from a private collection of crackling 78s. Other times you would find him in the sitting room, the air blue with smoke, watching the snooker or the showjumping on the television in the middle of the day with the curtains closed.

"I'm going up for ten minutes of a rest," he would say when the house got busy around him, as we tried to hustle him out into the fresh air.

"I'm not in good fettle myself. I could lie down too," my mother would respond. "It's time I got a bit selfish."

"I wondered when it would start."

"You're only interested in that cigarette."

"I'm going back up to bed, to get away from your tongue."

"Go where you'll get care."

On a mild day my father might stand on the front street for a while, with both hands on the wall around the garden. He stood looking out towards the beehives and, following the line of his sight, I was reminded of a time when he would sit on his hunkers for hours watching the bees come and go on the ramp in front of the hive. He liked to watch the young worker bees warming their bodies for flight, and the returning bees dancing for the hive: selflessly directing the other worker bees to a rich pollen find. But I think it was the patience and the courage of each small worker bee that he admired most. Small, exhausted bees resting after arrival, bright loaded pollen sacks on either side of their tired insect bodies. He knew the high angry buzz when a bee was upset and ready to sting, ready to die to protect the hive. And he took care to explain to us that in the bees' world the old drones were a burden on the store of honey and were put out of the hive to die before the winter.

Even when his wind was gone he would muster his strength when a swarm appeared. A tight grape-cluster of bees hanging on a branch, with the queen bee lodged somewhere in the middle. He would bring a large cardboard box and, without the protection of gloves or a veil, lower the stone weight of bees in a buzzing lump into the box and close the lid.

"A swarm in May is worth a load of hay,

A swarm in June is worth a silver spoon."

Now he stood gasping for air, searching the autumn fields with his big, straining, blood-vessel red eyes and airless face. His thoughts concentrated on his breathing: trying to loosen the knotted lump tied in his lungs. The rise and fall of his ribcage making heavy work out of taking in the air that was all around him.

"They'll lift that phlegm in the hospital for you," my mother had said to him, but we were on the brink of winter and we could see that he had no interest.

"The women will be all right," he'd say, leaving my mother to do the shopping, and ducking into Austie Wynne's pub for a pint of stout as soon as he had been fitted for a new jacket.

Daddy never wore a suit. He liked a sports jacket and a plain trousers. But he had to be dragged as far as the shops to have these occasional trousers and jackets bought for him. He wore a white shirt and a plain tie with a rub of Brylcream in his hair, and he liked a badge in his lapel: a small gold rose from a rosary prayer group or an Easter Rising commemorative paper lily held in place with a pin.

The cause was not important. There were Sinn Féin dances in the parish hall, and organised bus journeys to the border to fill in the craters in the unapproved roads dynamited by the British Army. And even though he had never really liked England when he had worked and lived there with my mother in the fifties he never took part.

He had been an active, outdoors man all his life and in England he had felt his individual freedom restricted. He mounted his own small rebellions. He poached the private lakes and rivers, snared game on the big estates, kept brown trout alive in the bathtub and brought them in damp, rolled newspapers on the back of a friend's BSA motorbike to let them breed in the wild in a small wood lake where they planned to fish undisturbed in the years to come.

"You can't be a rebel all your life," my mother would remind him every time he came in late from one of these poaching expeditions. "If you're going to get on in this world you have to conform sometime."

"You couldn't put manners on Paddy," he would smile in his defence, assuming his own obstinate nature to be a national virtue.

"'God is good, and the Devil isn't such a bad fellow either,' said the dying man to the priest, because it was no time to be making enemies," he'd joke with us.

I liked that. But I never really knew what his religious beliefs were. There was the rosary society badge in his lapel, of course, but that was for decoration. I had heard it mentioned that he had made a curiously pagan vow years ago, that if he was left his teeth he would not shave on a Sunday: he had good teeth. And he took us to Sunday mass only until we were ready to decide for ourselves what we believed. When I started kicking up a fuss he left me to my own devices. There was a holy Bible, a fat wad of flimsy, well-thumbed sheets between soft paper covers, on the shelf of the locker beside his bed. But good and bad, God and Devil, were for him, I think, forces of kindness or malice; idle gossip was always forbidden in the house.

"If you haven't anything good to say, then you shouldn't bother opening your mouth."

He kept a terrier for sport and he was good at tracking a single line of fox-prints in the snow back to a crevice in the mountain rocks on a winter's morning. Sending in the dog for a fox gone to earth. Freedom was a day in the fields with a gun, out in the snow-freshened air under an open blue sky. Blood heat in the chill of the morning.

On summer evenings after work he'd take a fibreglass rod with a spinning reel and walk down to the river to cast for a trout he had spotted rising near the bridge. He would light a cigarette and blow smoke to keep the midges away and tell yarns.

Yarns, the same yarns over again. The time he introduced several hand-reared clutches of pheasants to the valley.

"They have all my spuds scraped out of the ridges and eaten," a local farmer complained, stopping Daddy on the road.

"What sort of spuds are they?" he asked.

"Kerr's Pinks."

"The poor pheasants couldn't eat worse," he reassured the man, and went on his way.

The time a fog came down on the lake when they had Jim Early's boat out, but they had been able to make a straight line back to the shore by watching the line of the wake in the water behind the boat. How a sudden storm came up another night when they were out duck shooting and they pointed the boat into the waves and made for the shelter of an island where they waited out the storm with a brushwood fire and boiled gulls' eggs until the wind dropped. How Gus Flynn shot a pike from the bank using BB cartridges. The big fish got stuck on a sandbar and Gus waded in after it until the water was above his knees. When it came to just below his groin Gus turned back, shouting to the others: "I won't get the chemicals wet."

The fields brought out the best in him. And on patient walks with us as children he trained us to listen to the seed-pods of the wild broom bursting open in the summer heat. The simple things first. How to tell a rabbit from a hare, a red from a grey squirrel. To spot a gliding hawk drop fast on a young bird. To know that there were no weasels, only stoats in Ireland. Hedge-schooling us in the names of plants: the wild pea, also know as vetch, honeysuckle or the wild woodbine that gave off its perfume at night. Foxglove or fairy finger, also known as digitalis. Woodruff, dog daisy and eyebright.

"Daddy, you're a walking encyclopaedia," I said to him one time, and he was proud for both of us.

When we were bigger he took a younger brother and me to hazelwood and green oak glens to build shooting hides, and showed us how to camouflage our work with branches and ferns. Then we sat and waited like terrorists for the pigeon flocks coming in to roost on a windy evening. He trained us which shoulder to use, how to avoid the kick of the shot, and take down a sitting target or dare for a flying bird. Under his guidance I became an early riser trusted with a gun. Awake before the alarm clock and out without a breakfast, a shotgun on my arm – with the barrel always pointed at the ground – a red, Eley cartridge studded belt about my waist. Following a hungry fox out hunting the meadows in the early daylight. Its movements given away by the racketing magpies darting down around its head. Finding white feathers and a yellow leg, beak and red cock's-comb remains in the small pine plantation at the bridge by the railroad. The canny fox bettering my young running enthusiasm.

On the way home I was sure to spot a rabbit. Then I raised the shotgun and softly thumbed the hammer back. Levelled and took aim along the barrel using the studded sights. Three-in-one oil smell from the metal, fume of polish on the wooden stock. A killing tool that called up a heart-racing but concentrated calm. Soft pressure on the trigger, followed by the kick and blast of the exploding cartridge dented by the fall of the firing pin. A buck rabbit tumbled, kicked twice and lay still. His pelt scored with lead. The reek of cordite smoke and a spent cartridge popping under the ejector.

And when I knew how to hunt on my own, how to stalk

my quarry, wait under camouflage and make a profes-
sional kill, he took care to curb that power.

"Never point a gun at anyone, even if you know for
sure that the gun isn't loaded," he said, at pains to drum
into all our heads the shooting man's code of honour.
You can be dogged, yes. But no swagger, no exaggera-
tion, no shows of strength. Whether we were handling a
shotgun, tackling a new job, dealing with people or dealing with trouble: "A little bit of manners goes a long
way."

The star charts printed in the Saturday paper explaining
the heavens were cut out and kept. Lines that joined the
dotted stars into constellations memorised. My younger
brother, Owen, was soon out at night in a hooded
anorak, lying back against the ass-cart heeled-up to a
barn wall to pin-point Cassiopeia, Orion and the Plough,
also called the Big Dipper, Ursa Major, or the Great
Bear.

"Obstreperous," Daddy said, delighting in the sound of
the word. He enjoyed teasing the odd big word into our
vocabulary, though he was not a man for books.

He was a gardener by trade who wore his socks out
over his trousers. But he was inquisitive, progressive. He
never ate vegetables yet he liked to experiment, testing
new varieties of apple tree, strawberry plant and spud.
He dug over the ground so often with a spade that he
got a round lump of fluid on his knee. The stitched red
scar after the two operations ran the length of his leg. I
don't know precisely what happened, but I think that in-
jury and the crude method of its treatment, even the
time spent in the hospital, had a lasting effect on him.

"He was a bad patient," was all my mother would say.

We moved to my mother's home place soon after to
run the family farm. He still grew potatoes, cabbage-

plants and ridges of turnips and he introduced Charolais cattle to the farm when they were still new to the district. But he lost interest in gardening and he was never the same sportsman again. There were three boys in the family, and the older we grew the more jobs we were left. Each one of us he encouraged in turn.

Joseph, my older brother, had a yen for meddling with wind-up toys and clocks. Removing the curved glass faces and taking the blue main springs, the balance and golden cog-wheels out of the intricate frame.

Daddy found him a book called *The Junior Electrician,* which showed him how to make electromagnets from a nail and coiled copper wire. How to make crude microphones from the carbon bars out of old flashlamp batteries. When Joseph got a bit older my father loaded up an ass and cart with old valve radios and crystal sets left behind in a shed by a German refugee called Brock, who had made his living fixing radios and charging wet batteries during the war. The cattle were soon getting tangled in Joseph's experimental telephone wires and transmitter systems, which spanned the hedges and fields. My mother gave out about the danger to young calves.

"He has great brains," my father said in his defence.

I used to make model heads out of the blue daub from the ditches: a smooth stoneware clay that could be baked in the oven and then painted.

"Express yourself," was his advice to me when I started to script and draw my own action comics, and later followed my designs into art school.

"He's taken a sleeping tablet," my mother called down to me from her room. "He's ravelling a bit. Will you see to him?"

I had already heard her helping him down the stairs

and then back up again to his bedroom. After she got him up the stairs she sat with him for a while. When he was settled and breathing easy she went to her own bed. It must have been about two o'clock in the morning. I sat on in the chair in the front room, and a little later I heard him come back down the stairs again. This was unusual: he didn't like to take the stairs when he was so short in the breath.

He was sitting on the toilet, his trousers down around his ankles. The light was off. There was a bar of light from the hallway falling across the linoleum and I left him in peace for a while. When I looked in again several minutes later he was still sitting there.

I knew he was ill. But he had been in bad health for a long time. The doctor had said the same time last year that we would be lucky if we had him for the Christmas. He had been anointed then. And here he was, a year later, making his own way back from the toilet. It was just one more night of the year when he would lie awake, listening to the radio, coughing and smoking on the quiet, no matter how much we pleaded with him.

"I'm seeing things in my head," he said. "I don't know what's wrong."

"It's just the tablet making you dopey," I said. "You'll be all right when you lie down."

It crossed my mind that it might not have been wise to take that tablet. I settled him back in the bed. But he wouldn't lie down. I had to raise him up and stack the pillows behind his back. There was a smell of Brylcream and sweat and tobacco from the old brown jumper he wore sitting up in bed that night. He was not moaning or gasping, but what I thought was some sort of improvement in him was really just a sinking to a lower ebb.

It was after three o'clock in the morning, and it was just like putting a passively drunk man to bed.

I came back later and he appeared to be dozing. His breathing sounded better and I laid him back in the bed. I was about to leave the room when he woke up. He wanted to be propped up again. I thought he was being a bit awkward: if he just lay down quietly he would soon drop off and get a good night's sleep. But I came back and propped him up with extra pillows so that he could sleep sitting up. I guessed that he would light a cigarette the minute I left the room.

I looked in one more time before going to bed. His eyes were closed and he was nodding his head.

"Ah, Bernard, Bernard, he's gone. Ah, Bernard. He's gone on us."

He was sitting up in the bed exactly where I had left him, and my mother was there standing over him. I put my hands on his two shoulders. He slumped forward, and when I eased him back he felt heavy and cold. The hands were colder still.

"Ah, why didn't I stay with him? What tempted me to go to bed?" my mother said.

I put my two hands on his chest and pumped the lungs. There was a groan. But it was only trapped air in the lungs.

"O God, Daddy."

It was somewhere between five and six o'clock in the morning. I said I would get dressed and go for help. I laid my father out straight in the bed and crossed his arms, but I did not cover his face. Then I left my mother alone with him in the bedroom. When I was ready to go she was getting dressed in her own room.

The birds were just beginning to squabble. There was a cold grey fog and a faint light in the air. The features of the countryside were still dark. I went directly to my brother's house: a brown bungalow with a network of television, commercial and citizen-band radio aerials bolted on the chimneys. I tapped with a bare knuckle on the bedroom window-pane and called softly. He came to the front door and I spoke to him from the porch.

"It's Daddy," I said.

I drove into the village and knocked on the door of the priest's house. There was no answer. The world I had known at the hour of his death had changed. The dawn light increasing, a car on the move in the valley. I felt I had been away a long time. I went to the lit village telephone kiosk to try telephoning the priest. I got through straight away and he said he would be there as soon as he was dressed. On my way out of the kiosk I met a police car. Three uniformed guards in the back and a detective with an Uzi submachine gun in his lap sitting beside the driver. They wanted to know my business.

The priest had been up to the room, said the necessary prayers and left. Joseph's wife Catherine and Owen's wife Susan set about tidying the house. We could expect callers soon and it was time for Owen, Joseph and myself to go upstairs to the room to shave, wash and dress the corpse.

The flesh was getting colder by the hour. I looked at the body with no real sense that Daddy was still there: the thought of some presence, some awareness remaining on in the vicinity of the corpse was far too horrible to consider.

We went about the business of washing our dead father in a practical way. The odd groan of air still came from his lips. But we were level-headed, manly, determined. Traits he had taught us. Following his example by doing what must be done. Courage of a man with a single hayfork facing into a big open field of meadow. Trained to the feel of warm afterbirth from a cow calving. Or doing away with a barrelful of sheepdog pups in the hayshed by drowning or hitting their heads off a stone. I scrubbed his face with a cloth. We took turns with a bowl of water and a razor. Joseph clipped his fingernails and cleaned back years of nicotine stains.

He was sixty-four. Death had made him look younger. There was no strain anymore, and the features of his face were calm, now that he had been released from that awful struggle for breath. We dressed him in his good wool sports jacket, plain brown trousers, white shirt, plumb-stone tie.

"Thanks be to God we don't use shrouds anymore," Owen said, after we had put a board under the mattress to raise him up in the bed. "Imagine if you had to go around the next world in a brown shroud with a holy picture pasted on the front, like an old concert tour T-shirt. You'd look ridiculous."

We were relieved to have the job done.

The first people to arrive after the priest on that grey autumn morning were Andy and Joan Murray, a couple of neighbours with a young family who lived near the farm of land we had over the road. They were practical and thoughtful and they wanted to fix breakfast for all of us.

Afterwards, Joseph and Owen left the house to visit the undertakers, to see about the coffin and the burial plot. I sat down and wrote the death notice for tomorrow's paper.

HENRY Michael (Arigna) – Nov 6th, 1987, at his residence, deeply regretted by his loving wife, Marian, his sons Joseph, Bernard and Owen, daughters-in-law Catherine and Susan, grandson David, sisters Mary and Kathleen, brother Terry, brothers-in-law, sisters-in-law, nieces and nephews, relatives and friends. Rest in Peace. Removal from house Saturday 7th, arrive church of Immaculate Conception (Arigna) at 7 o'clock. Funeral after 11 o'clock mass, to Kilronan Cemetery.

The hands of the clock were slow to surrender the hours. We had callers all day but it was in the evening that the neighbours began crowding in. The more people appeared the more numbing every dry handshake and well-meant "sorry for your trouble" became. And my own attempts to remember the name or the face along with the automatic "thank you". I stood in the hallway with Uncle Joe, my mother's younger brother. I knew that he had always liked my father and he was finding it a long day. By the time it got dark we had to get out of the house.

"Do you need any messages?" Uncle Joe asked the others.

"No," said Catherine.

"Are you sure? Not even a mineral?"

"No."

"Oh, for God's sake can't you let the man go for a pint," Joan Murray said. "He can bring back a few minerals."

If the people in the bar were surprised to see us they did not show it. Andy Murray was there and the chat was about the hunt for Dessie O'Hare, the man known as the Border Fox. He had shot his way out of one police barracks already and was still on the loose despite a nationwide manhunt, the armed police checkpoints everywhere you went, and the roving dawn patrols.

"Your father never had much to say to the guards," Uncle Joe said.

"*Ná bí ag caint*," I said, my father's words coming back to me.

"Say nothing and keep saying it," Uncle Joe said, wiping a tear away.

The Big Dipper was over our heads, and outside we remembered the clippings out of the Saturday papers, and happier nights walking home under the stars.

Back at the house again, Owen and myself brought two kitchen chairs up to the bedroom and got ready to stay awake all night, keeping the traditional vigil over the corpse.

"If we really want to keep Daddy company we should have a constant supply of Woodbines burning in the ashtray and the clock radio turned up," Owen said.

We didn't go that far, but sitting on in the room Owen, Uncle Joe and myself had a few hot whiskeys, drank beer from the neck of the bottle and told yarns. We weren't the type to recite prayers all night over the corpse, and my father would not have been the type to listen. Owen had a story Joan Murray had told earlier. She used to worry about an ass breaking into our field at the side of her house. She put out the animal several times but he kept coming back. Finally she met my father.

"The old ass has to eat too," he said complacently. "Instead of putting him to the road, why don't you give the children a spin on his back? The ass would have his bite to eat. You have the run of the field and the children would love the spin."

It was after three o'clock in the morning, but Andy Murray came up the stairs to join us. We were soon back to the hunt for the Border Fox.

"I met a patrol this morning," I said. "I think they were watching a house. I was annoyed with them when they stopped me. My mother was waiting here on her own. But they couldn't have known my father was dead, and I thought of what Daddy always said, 'a little bit of manners ...' They were a help in the end. They sent a message on the radio, and got a neighbour to break the news to Owen."

"They were better off helping you than chasing the Fox," Andy Murray said. "How is any detective wearing a big sheepskin coat and his best leather shoes going to catch a wanted man running across a bog in a string vest and a pair of wellingtons? I saw an armed detective on the bridge in Carrick-on-Shannon the other day and he had that many coats on him he couldn't lift his arms."

We were left off when Joseph and Catherine returned to the house, their children seen to, shortly before eight o'clock the next morning.

I couldn't sleep. I changed into working clothes, built up the fire in the kitchen and cleaned the ashes out of the grate in the front room; then went outside to do whatever jobs had to be done. The day was calm. The air stone-grey. Chalk-dust haze and dry remains of leaves underfoot in the yard, around the hayshed and the barns. Pheasant weather. Perfect for roaming the fields with a gun.

This was the longest day of all. The house like a tomb with the stone rolled over the top, muted and enclosed in grief.

Journeys were made out of the house in the evening to call on the men digging the grave. I went out to the graveyard with a load of sandwiches, stout and whiskey. They had met a terrible rock and they had been hammering away in turns at this mud-lodged and intractible stone for hours. Owen and Joseph were there amongst the in-laws and neighbours, working with a sledge hammer in the wet bottom of the grave.

We were standing about eating and taking turns at the bottle when the retired doctor who owned the big house overlooking the lake arrived. He stood a minute by a headstone in another part of the graveyard and then he came over to us. He said it was mild and I made some remark about the midges being at me, although it was the month of November.

"You must be using the wrong shampoo," the doctor said.

"I was going to say the shampoo he used couldn't be great," Andy Murray said, watching the doctor's bald head retreating. "A wipe of the sponge for him."

"There was plenty of men looking at their wellingtons when he came out with that one," Owen said, and we laughed together and passed the bottle around again. When we turned back to the rock in the grave we saw that a hair-line crack had appeared. A stroke of the hammer broke the stone in two.

The split-hinged bannisters at the top of the stairs were removed to make room for the coffin. The neighbours gathered to say the rosary, kneeling around the bedroom and out on the landing. Then it was time for us to leave him into the coffin. A last sight of the corpse before the coffin was lidded. A moment worse than finding him dead in the room. The screws shaped like small crosses set in line for that moment of fixing down the lid, a moment for which there is no consolation.

With the lid in place and the last prayers said we brought the coffin out onto the front street. A crowd of people waiting there: low voices, scuffling feet. I carried the coffin alongside my Uncle Joe, cousins and brothers. With equal care we shifted the weight off our shoulders and loaded the coffin into the back of the hearse waiting in the lane. We left an aunt behind in the house and then set out for the church. There were a lot of cars by the side of the road waiting to join the cortège.

"A good man."

"Likeable."

"A wit."

"A drinker."

"Comical sort."

A big crowd gathered outside the chapel, waiting to show their respect. Lined up in the front seat with the family I half-heard a reading from the Gospel and a notice for the Credit Union read out after holy communion.

The priest sprinkled holy water with a besom over the coffin. I watched the specks of clear water gleam on the varnished wood in the chapel light. On the lid of the coffin the words "Rest in Pease" were engraved on a brass plaque, the word peace mistakenly spelled with an S. A detail that would not have escaped Daddy. I pictured him giving me the wink.

"*Ná bí ag caint*. The undertaker has to make a living, too."

A Perfect Quiet

FOR A WHILE I THOUGHT I felt a presence, a spirit trace of the last occupant in the house. A rented cottage in the north-west of Ireland: solitary, south-facing, with a dry flagstone front street, deep stone-built walls, three rooms and a chilly bathroom under a corrugated iron roof, painted green. Standing in the front porch you can see the lights of the nearest small town on the night-time horizon, but coming up the flood-torn boreen to the house, in the roaring silence of this empty countryside, you might think my chimney was on fire because of that orange glow behind the leaves that screen merchant roofs and church steeple.

My neighbours are all old country people, grown used to this empty quiet. Like the famished bachelor up the road who said to me the other day: "I don't smoke, drink or eat hay. I'm a friend to neither man nor beast."

The growling sheepdog farms that surround the house are all maintained by ample women with tiny, chesty husbands. In the mornings the women are up before seven, opening henhouse doors. Running in hungry looking mother cows and fat yearlings from the fields. Milking Friesians in midge-eaten summer barns. Carrying baled hay to the outliers when the white frost is on the grass. Hoisting creamery cans up on long trailers and then driving the gap-churning and mud-flinging big back-wheel tractors to the crossroads. Lighting ash-filled and cinder-packed Rayburns with soda bread baking-ovens and air-locked hot-water pipes. Hanging out fanfares of washing, fields of sheets and pillowcases, tea-towels, jumpers and overalls flapping in the breeze before the church bell strikes eleven. Then the husbands rise, fishing stubby cigarette ends out of tobacco-smelling pockets, the heels trespassing out of their socks, foot-printing the freshly washed floor and coughing into the coal bucket. They lean over black iron frying pans searching for boxty and fried rasher breakfasts.

"Will you sit down and I'll fix a bite to eat for you," a wife bustles. "You have me up the walls just looking at you."

The routine of the day in progress.

Death has thinned out the old parish, leaving the smallest holdings and empty cottages to the auctioneers. Colour photographs soon appear in the windows, advertising remote homes in need of repair. A burden on nephews and relations away in London or America; swept out and sold for holiday cottages to Continentals, drifters, strays.

The summer cottages to let bring strange arrivals: separated couples, territorial Germans nailing up no trespassing signs, green-fingered Dutch women in a haze of potted geraniums. Hairy-knuckled potters and organic gardeners. Stone polishers, jewellers, candlemakers and baggy trousered photographers doing cookery books.

When I moved in the owners had fitted carpet tiles and curtains, and left behind a threadbare settee and an armchair, both oversized and impossible to remove.

The windows had been given a new coat of hardgloss and there were recent white paint splashes on the front street. But in every room I found left-over tokens of another's lifetime. Hints of pipesmoke and a smell of old working clothes. Musted newspapers and magazines going back years. Holy pictures in frames, with dust behind the glass. Medals and special prayers in plastic envelopes. Almanacs listing marts and fair days. And a faded paper icon with the words: "I will bless the house in which the picture of my sacred heart shall be exposed and honoured."

I bring new oddments in their place. A word processor and a ream of typing paper. A jar full of biros, felt-tips and paper-clips.

Dreams at night of falling through space.

Then the month of April comes in: days of big skies, triumphant rainbows, thunderstorm clouds boating across navy blue horizons. The silence of the house after hard-hitting hailstones on the corrugated iron roof.

I find it hard to recall that hollow feeling in the stomach when I first looked in the clouded windows of this locked cottage and wondered if I could rent it at a good price. The place was strange and new; its smells, creaks, draughts, off-centre lights in the wooden ceiling, second-hand furniture, new bed, and the taste of the tap water were alien to me.

Slowly I came to know the warped board and leaning character of this generations-deep place. The old man or baby noises the house made at night. The sound of the rain on the window-panes and the wind in the tops of the trees. The calling of the curlews and the gloating snipe on the open bog below the house. The clatter and scrape of crows on the iron roof, the splutter of an overflowing gutter, the passing of a tractor outside, the gurglings in the cistern, and the smell of wet soot in the front room after I had been away for a few days. Now, these are all parts of the natural undercurrent of the place, soothing and familiar signs that everything is in order about the house.

I can stumble into these silently waiting rooms in complete darkness and grope for the old round, black bakelite switches without being nervous or afraid. I trust this place. This is my home. My spaceship cottage with its own life-support system. Its shelves full of books, a continental quilt on the bed, Van Morrison records in a long playing vinyl collection going back fifteen years. A wobble in the saucepan handles, and a rattling collection of empty wine bottles stacked on top of the press. Muddy footprints and a pair of walking boots in the front porch.

I live quietly here, locked into a private orbit of my own working routines. Passing neighbours talk about the weather. The radio and the postman are the only proof of a larger world.

When I get restless I shove a short-hand notepad in my pocket and leave my space cabin to take long and inquisitive walks through the fields, covering miles of canal, river and forest paths. Breathing in the calm, pine-scented air, the sweet smell of the flowering whin bushes, the perfume of wild rockets in the water meadows. Following the hare-runs to find a grassy track across the bog below the house, and making it my own among skylarks. And in the fine weather I hike out past the town to the mountains beyond to walk that Stone Age hill country, with its secretive moon- and sun-aligned and polar star monuments.

May sees a snowfall of white flowering blossom on every hawthorn. Bluebells flood the wood floor.

I stop to give an ear to an old boy sitting on the ditch,

giving instructions to the missis, digging manure into the cabbage patch. He tells me: "She's the best little worker ever put an arm out through the sleeve of a coat."

And then he stoops down on his hunkers in the shelter of the primrose ditch-back to light up a cigarette from a box of Navy Cut Players, to recount his improbable better days. And how the neighbour who used to live in my cottage was never the same after falling twenty feet off a ten foot ladder.

"His brain shifted after the fall," he says. "I can't say where it was before, but it was no use to him at all after that."

The rain fell all through the month of July. A drenching mizzle in the hedgerows, cloaking distant landmarks. Wisps of cloud in the conifer plantations and the rampant, purple rhododendron on the hills. The summer growth rank and water-swollen. The misted fields brimming with meadow buttercup and wild yellow iris flowers.

There are long weeks of humiliation in the rain. My faith is worn away by the constant downpour, and I begin to feel it has been an ill-judged move to such a remote cottage in this half-mad part of the country.

I can hardly remember a day when I could throw open the windows to let out the used air in the house. When the breeze lifted the curtains and blew down the postcards on the window sill. But the breeze never carried the scent of new-mown hay, and never a hint of honeysuckle perfume in the moth-hours. No butterflies, no grasshoppers, no cuckoo spit on the long grass. The farmers made muddy silage in the rain.

If the sun found its bright strength for a day I brought out an armchair and sat by the front porch. Dappled sun in the lane. Morning light glimmering through the leaves. Dog rose, sweet briar and wild strawberries in the hedgerows and the sun-warmed ditches. A blue-jean sky.

On these special days I put on a clean white shirt and a broad-brimmed straw hat to shade the rising pages of the manuscript of an ambitious first novel. A coffee mug perched on the window ledge.

I was lured away from the cottage by a girl who arrived at the back end of the summer. She was town lights and people. But our affair was inevitable and headlong. We started to meet in the evenings after I finished my day's work at the writing table. Then days went missing. There was always a party somewhere, or a group of friends going back to a different town house. Round-up of coins for the cigarette machine, arms loaded with bottles of spirits and beer. It would be five or six in the morning before the party broke up.

I loved the early stages of the affair. Past the trials of courtship and on to the intimacy of drinking together in stone-floor and wood-panelled pubs. Heads bent close together over a menu, laughing over our table manners. Confident and easy together. A sense of weightlessness. And that sensual closeness and low honeymoon light on the quilt and her raised bare shoulder above the covers in the bedroom in the long mornings.

We were happy then, but in the grey half-light before dawn in early September we split up. The affair over. We had paced around the one room all night, our talk ending with those tired words: "I hope we can still be friends."

Out on the pavement I fitted the strap of a full-face helmet under my chin, climbed up on a motorbike and drove back hard for the country. I felt as cold as a blade cutting through the new morning, heading for home at full throttle. The stars winked out in clusters. The light of rising day on the horizon. Tomcats slipped into ditches and rainbow-coloured cock pheasants, startled by my sudden appearance around a bend, shuddered and flung themselves with whistling tail feathers into the air as the small birds raised their dawn outcry. The autumn floods drained away and the winter gales came in early. Haws and hard black sloes and damson fruits in the hedgerows. Ragged hardwoods. The air full of leaves. Sluggish wasps and cooking apples in the orchard grass. Spoil of mildew on the blackberries. The wild plum bitter after the frost. Then the ice grew like crystal ferns on the insides of empty room windows. The parties were over and there was no more girl. Only a brown hare with large, human eyes who visited the front street of my cottage. The paint now peeling off the window frames and washed away from the once white walls.

When the clocks were put back an hour, and the early dark winter evenings came in, I eased myself off the motorbike, my fingers in pain, my body stiff and numb with the bite of the freezing air. And the first job was to light the open fire in the front room so that it would be going strong by the time I had the dinner cooked. The cheerless cold giving way to the warm blend of wood smoke and beef stew, with carrots, basil and onions simmering in the kitchen. When I had the money to spare I set a ritual bottle of red wine to warm by the fire, so that it tasted rich and full with the food. I swallowed the first glass quickly and waited for the rush of warmth to spread through my body. With a good dinner put away, the radio playing low, the fire going well and it below zero outside, and sipping a final glass of wine, I could settle into the ancient but hugely comfortable armchair for the night, break open a packet of foolscap paper, uncap a clear biro, my mind a private debating chamber.

The full moon in its high winter station. Whooping

swans flying over the house. Snow lines on the rim of the mountains. Sharp air frost, and a ring of cloud vapour around the base of the hills, invisibly suspended over the lake water. A luminous world in strong moonlight. Tranquil, ageless, perfected.

It feels like this long winter should be over by now. My book is finished and an embarrassment. There is no woman. The fire makes soft whispers as it settles into embers. I am drowsy and half-asleep in my armchair with the radio playing when there is an interruption in the regular programme. The announcer states that the American space shuttle is passing over the country. There will be a live radio link-up with the crew in their cabin in the next few minutes. With the volume on the radio turned up I step outside my back door to search the night sky. I see it. There in the north. Racing past the constellations at nine times the speed of sound. Radio silence. Then, a bleep, and the astronauts' voices crackling with static echo inside the house. I stand alone in the dark at my back door, connected to that bright head of light, riding on the slipstream one hundred miles out from earth. Uplift of the imagination. Though the speeding light soon meets the horizon and our link over the airwaves is broken. Turning back into the house I think I might never again know such perfect quiet, such perfect belief. Or feel so at home in the world.

Cuckoo Visits

I'VE TOLD CATHY SHE CAN expect a two-storey farmhouse on the side of the mountain, set down among
stone-built sheds at the end of a trimmed hawthorn
lane, and surrounded by hilly fields so steep you could
hang pictures on them.

Cathy will be meeting my mother for the first time: a
small woman with a delft teapot in one hand and a cotton scarf tied around her head, running from the
scullery – we call it the back kitchen – to the hot, number
eight black Stanley range in the kitchen, making endless
journeys to and fro, to set the table and to wet the tea.

"There is always a cup of tea for a visitor, or a drop of
whiskey if there's a heel left in the bottle. That's what my
mother says," I tell Cathy, as she brushes a stray curl out
of her eyes.

I have extra bits of shopping in my bag, bought in the
town this morning: pasta, a tin of sweetcorn, cucumber,
cream cheese with herbs, a chocolate and pineapple log.
Exotic additions only. My mother will already have a
high tea made, left out in the back kitchen under a clean

tea-towel, ready to be served. Home-made brown bread.
An apple or a rhubarb tart. Slices of ham folded in rolls
on a bed of lettuce from her own garden, with short
green scallions pulled a bit too soon. Tomatoes too. But
not salad cream. She's been to America to see her sister
and she prefers mayonnaise.

Cathy is an independent sort: a good job in town, a mi-
crowave oven and her own car. But we have been going
out together for a year and we have reached the point
where we can usually guess what the other one is thinking.

We drive in silence and the roads are so familiar I take
it for granted that Cathy knows the last bit of the way. I
offer no directions, we go past the turn, and have to re-
verse back.

Cathy waves to the car coming behind. We have two
Dutch friends tailing us in their own car: two sisters in
their late seventies, Constance and Jeannette. Both
women have the hallmarks of great beauty in their youth.
Jeannette is a fresh-faced woman with a clear light in her
eyes. She has a knowing, travelled and self-effacing manner. Constance has a broach at her neck, wears fine
woollen cardigans and has the more brusque, aristocratic
manner.

"You should change your hair," she said to Cathy
shortly after they met. "Pick a good salon. Ask their advice. That's their job. Don't try to save money. Not on
your hair."

I met Constance through her niece when I was travelling in the Netherlands. I've lost touch with the niece,
but Constance and myself have remained friends. When
she arrived in Ireland last year I tried to repay her kindness in the Netherlands with a good impression of my
homeplace. She met my mother on that visit.

"Your mother is wonderful," Constance said afterwards. "And so lively, too."

Now she wants her sister to share her enthusiasm. Their motives are perfectly sincere, but for me they are a further proof that these small holdings in the West of Ireland have only a curiosity value in the new Europe. For Cathy the pair of older women visitors are a welcome smokescreen.

I telephoned earlier in the week to warn my mother we would be calling. She would never forgive me if we caught her with the curlers in her hair, the sheets of newspaper left down on the kitchen floor after mopping, the loaf of bread or the waxed-paper litre of milk and a side plate with potato skins waiting to be cleared from the table.

I direct the cars in the gate and see that the two stone piers have a new coat of paint. My mother comes out to meet us on the front street. We stop beside her recently fitted Georgian windows. A small, mongrel terrier, bunty-tailed and bent in two, barks and then scuffles a welcome around our feet.

"She's as ugly as sin, but she has a great little personality," my mother says. "The coldest dog in Ireland," she adds. "She pushes past me in the morning to get in at the electric heater. Takes all the heat. People would have me locked up if they saw me passing down a tasty bit of chicken to that dog in the morning that would do my own dinner. But she's company for me when I'm here on my own at night."

She talks non-stop as she leads us down the cement front street.

The green-cylinder push-mower has been in use on the shaved lawn. Her daffodil and crocus flower beds are just coming into bloom. The greenhouse in the corner of the garden is stacked with polystyrene trays of sprouting broccoli and flower seeds. And her "little man", a bare-bellied cement cherub, stands in the other corner beside the conifer and heather bed, shouldering a bowl of primulas. A bushy azalea in a red earthenware pot is on display outside the porch.

"I've looked after it like a baby all winter," my mother says, when the women remark on the strong white blooms. "In and out with it at night when there's a sign of frost. Slamming doors at all hours and waking up the neighbours."

There is a warm fire of windfall elm and peat briquettes in the sitting room, which we have always called the lower room. The ladies are settled in big second-hand Dutch furniture chairs around the tiled fireplace. I seat Cathy on the sofa, leaving my mother to do all the talking.

After being complimented on her house she confides to the visitors that she has a great interest in old stately homes and fine gardens. Powerscourt is lovely, but she tells Constance how she visited Bunratty castle with a sister once and, looking over the medieval interior she had remarked: "Bejesus, me own place is better than this."

I round up glasses from the china cabinet where the ornaments we bought for her as children are kept, and take the glasses to the back kitchen to pour a beer for myself, whiskey for the visitors and a sherry for my mother. I bring the drinks in on a tray. The glasses are raised and: "*Sláinte.*"

My mother says that Constance and Jeannette are a picture of health. They put it down to good fortune more than money, easy times or good living. And my mother is reminded of a story about an old woman of eighty, living up the road, who told a visiting doctor she had neither an ache nor a pain despite her age, although at times her mind might wander a bit. When the doctor asked what kind of food she had eaten over the years, she said:

"Anything I was given."

Constance, having met my mother before, has a little yarn of her own ready.

"Jesus, Mary and Joseph were having a discussion about what places they would most like to visit if they were given a chance to return to this earth. Joseph said he'd love to go back to Nazareth to spend a day in the little carpenter's shop he'd had there. Jesus said he often longed to go back to the serenity and the peace he found around the sea of Galilee. Mary said that she'd love to pay a visit to the shrine at Knock, because she'd never been there before."

"I left my hand on the spot where the apparition appeared," my mother says. "I used to have terrible pins and needles up and down my arm. The night after I got back I thought the pain in my arm was worse than ever. But when I woke up in the morning the pain was gone. It never came back."

Constance opens a shopping bag and produces a present for my mother: a framed photograph of a Marian Year shrine.

"I'm a great believer in the Blessed Virgin," my mother says, admiring the gift. "She always answers my prayers."

"The Irish are all great believers, I think, in the Blessed Virgin," Jeannette says.

"They're great believers in holy mothers, all round," I add.

"Is it true that Irish men don't get married until late in life?" Jeannette asks.

"Married is it?" my mother says. "Why should they get married when Mammy does all? They have the times of Molly Bán, with mothers dancing attendance on them."

"There's an old joke that says Jesus must have been an Irishman, because his mother thought he was Christ Almighty," I tell Jeannette.

"Don't listen to him. There's no religion in this fella," my mother says, leaving the photograph on the mantelshelf. "They take that from their father, poor Michael..." the words trail off.

"I miss him," she says, when Cathy probes. "He was a very quiet sort of a man. Too quiet, maybe. All I have against him is that he smoked himself to death. It was a selfish thing to do. He wasn't thinking about the rest of us. There's an awful emptiness now."

The dog stretches out in its accustomed place on the rug in front of the fire.

In this lull, Jeannette asks my mother if she has any regrets.

"It was a hard life," she says. "I always felt I had it hard, or at least I was always working for someone else, or taking care of someone. I took care of my father when he got sick, and I looked after their father, poor Michael, until the end. I'm glad I did that. And I'm glad that I kept the promise I made to my own father to always look after the farm when he was gone."

I go to the back kitchen to make up fresh drinks. Then I leave my mother chatting with the two older women and take Cathy out around the back of the house.

Familiar cow piss smell in the yard, strong about the dung-heap at the back of the barns. Last year's weather-brown bales scattered about the pitted dirt and hayseed floor of the shed.

The machinery is left up under the roof and out of the weather as soon as we empty a bay in the shed. The saw-blade and pointed fingers on the arm of the mowing machine raised and fastened. Black prongs missing from the yellow and green hayflash. The cocklifter sitting on its back. The machinery silent and stiff with rust and tired grease after a winter of neglect.

The grey diesel twenty tractor stands in the lane, as little used as the rest, waiting for the summer.

I have already been back home for a week in April to fence off the meadows. Putting the cattle out of the meadows marks the start of the working year. Even for a man it is hard, sweating work, but it is essential for the survival of the farm. Sinking the pine fencing posts with a spade and crowbar. Stretching the barbed-wire across the gaps, using a claw-hammer with a loose handle. Bushing the breaks in the ditches with a bow-saw and hedge-knife.

The meadows are always fenced off late and it will be the end of June before we will begin to watch the weather and consider giving the machinery an overhaul. We will wait for the long-range weather forecast on the BBC, and when their computer charts, satellite photos and isobars say that the Gulf Stream has edged into northern waters, and a ridge of high pressure is on the way, we will make hay.

We all pull together, two brothers and myself, and sometimes a neighbouring cousin, arriving back to the farm each year to get the job done. A queue of cars with baby chairs in the back parked in the lane. The rush on. Dispatches for diesel and extra shopping. The tractor started with a run on the hill. It stands with the engine ticking over while we pump each machine nipple with black grease, fuel the two-gallon tank and fill the radiator with water from the well. The smell of farm diesel strained through an old pair of nylons and hot machine fumes rising in the sunlit morning air while the dew is drying off the grass. My two brothers will do the cutting in turns, being better tractor drivers than me, and I will do the shaking of the three big meadows we call the first, second and third fields. Working against the clock and the whims of the weather to get all the hay saved in one big sweep.

The hay will have to be cut, shaken three or four times and then gathered into wind-rolls for the baler. And despite the labour and the upset of it all there is a solid, good feeling when we hear the regular, rasping iron-lung thump of the baler working in the field, racing in laps as it works towards the middle. Square bales falling out of the back chute. Parcels of fodder that will lie for a night and a day in the field and will then be ferried to the hayshed in small loads of twelve or fourteen on the cock-lifter, with a man sitting on the bonnet of the tractor to keep the front wheels on the ground.

The reward is a hayshed stacked to the rafters with good bales, smelling of dry grass seasoned without rain, and safe under a roof for the winter. In between we've had evenings in the pub after a punishing day in the meadow field. The pan has been taken down for late night fry-ups in the kitchen; breakfasts and dinners cooked for us by a mother seeing we have everything. Boisterous, loud men together, grown big and elbowing in around the crowded table, with my mother doing the fussing and the feeding; the food tasting as familiar and as good as always.

We've had panics over broken machine parts, rain clouds at the butt of the wind. Uneasy waits for the man with the baler to arrive. Sunburn and sore fingers lifting nylon-cord-tied bales. But if the weather holds the work is done in less than two weeks and we can break up with a burden lifted and go back to wives and jobs, back to other towns and other concerns.

I walk with Cathy out the first field through a pollen-smelling, ankle-high new growth of black-topped ribwort and bluebells rising in the spring meadows. The hawthorn hedges are in green leaf, with just a week or so to wait for their bridal veils of white blossom. I point out views to Cathy, name lakes and mountains and the bright gables of surrounding towns. Then I show her the margins of the farm.

"So your mother runs things by herself when you're not here?" Cathy says.

"She has what she calls a programme left out for herself. It keeps her busy. The other brothers look in on her. She navigates all right on her own. She knows more about the animals than the rest of us put together. We keep the herd number down to what she can manage."

"Isn't it hard work for her?"

"It's what she wants. She'd rather be out cutting a field of weeds, working in her garden or looking after cattle than be stuck in the house all day."

"Would you consider taking over?"

"Right now the place is on hold. If it's not losing money it's certainly not making any. With our help my mother can still manage, but I don't think any one of us wants to be tied down to the place."

"You could let the place."

"Family pride," I tell her.

We sit on the side of a dry ditch, out of the wind, deep in birdsong and sunlight, saying nothing. Then we hear a cuckoo balanced on an ESB wire: hooded grey and home again on a summer visit. We listen to its stammering cuckoo calls until the bird swoops away, with two small birds following on its tail.

Tea is ready in the kitchen. The tablecloth is off for the visitors to see the shine and polished wood of the dining table. Cathy smiles at me when she sees the ham, tomatoes, lettuce and young scallions I told her would be there. The two sisters are already seated, my mother has the teapot in her hand. I look things over and find she's forgotten the butter.

"I'm sure you two have great fun when you're

together," Cathy says.

"We do," I tell her.

My mother won't join us at the table. She hurries and fusses and runs with fresh cups of tea in her hand, seeing that everybody is looked after.

Cathy asks her about my other brothers.

"Both married and gone," she says, looking at me. "There's only this fella left."

"It's only natural that they leave," Constance reassures her, smiling at Cathy. "They outgrow the nest. It's worse if they don't go. Leaving is a good thing. Like planting out your seedlings. It toughens them up."

My mother says nothing.

Constance and Jeannette beg my mother to sit down, but it is only when we are finishised eating, and sitting back with second cups of tea, that my mother perches at the end of the table with a small plate to share a bite with us. After the meal it is time to leave. The two older women say that they would prefer not to have to drive after dark.

I show the visitors the best way to turn in the drive and my mother, who has never driven a car in her life, tells Cathy to be sure to take the lane in first gear.

A commotion starts when my mother sees the cattle with their young suck-calves at their heels, wandering into the lane ahead of the cars. She halts the traffic and runs the hill to herd the slow-moving cattle out of the way.

"I think your mother panicked," Cathy says, watching her hurry the calves into the front pasture.

The dog takes after the back wheels of the cars when we start to move off. We make parting waves through the windows, and looking back in the rear-view mirror I see her standing there on the front street beside her flowering azalia as I lead the visitors out the gate.

After the Festival

I N THE FRONT BAR OF a public house in a tidy village
with only one street and no work, time sits like the
publican, Stephen McGettigan, an open mouth
glued to the television. His eyes glazed over; the reflections of the daytime cartoons flickering in his sticky
thumb-printed glasses. His mind as vacant as his carpark.
Flat pints yellow on the bartop, and nobody will ever
want petrol again from the pump with the label saying
you have to multiply the prices by two, until someone re-
sets the tumblers.

A windy day outside, made of thin sunlight and foot-
loose, dusty disappointment. A day of chilly frustration
before the cold ashes of empty grates that can send a
body drinking too soon to hope for a happy outcome.
No good could come of going drinking this windy day,
when all the world is off somewhere, going someplace
more interesting in a warm car.

Stink sheep trespass in the close conifer mountains
above, and for the town traders below every day is a half-
day with a long lunch-break – the brown doors are bolt-

ed well before one o'clock, and it is late after two before the nylon shop-coated and balding merchants return to their quiet humming freezers, cold-rooms and hanging banners of fly-paper.

Along the hawthorn country roads branching out either side of the village the blinds are down on the private holiday cottages owned by remote Germans. At the start of the lanes the letterboxes stand like rusty navigation poles on wild stretches of pock-bitten, patched and pot-holed again tarmac roads.

Legs outstretched and half-asleep, McGettigan dreams back to the roaring days when every bar for miles around had an extension out the back. Big singing lounges built on to old pub gables – coloured bulbs in the eaves, and low-walled, stony half-acre carparks. He had four bar-girls on every night, taking orders between the packed tables, carrying pint glassfuls of notes and change. Every day he oiled the tray of his till for the Sunday-suited and summer dressed couples on the rip: empties stacked higher than the great pyramids of Egypt, and new orders brought on round trays with a thirsty trout on the bottom.

A different band every night in the singing lounges that sprang up on these flat bog-cotton plains. Like settler towns rising on the open prairies of the Wild West frontier. It was the heyday of smiling country drummers tapping endless one ... two ... three, one ... two ... threes. Tan cowboy-booted bandsmen, with short denim jackets worn with the collar turned up. Yamaha electric organs on thin metal legs squeezed and pecked at by vodka and white women with high hair-dos. Cheerful men pumping scarlet accordions to their hearts' content. And a jolly singer in a beer-gut stretched and more frilly than a field of boochallawns shirt, singing all the old come-all-yous. Dairy farmers, council workers, post and telegraph men, civil servants and schoolteachers, moonlighting in estate wagons loaded to the axle with speakers, mike-stands and amplifiers. Pub bandsmen criss-crossing the country at twilight to their regular engagements, advertised in the small boxes that filled the inside back pages of every local paper.

An audience made up of boom-times builders, block-layers, and men a week on the beer. Women who could hold their drink, even if they couldn't hold a note, sending up requests for themselves to sing. Arm-locked mothers out on the floor, swinging or jiving together. And small, neat old boys in brown suits with shining faces, whiskey breaths and the free travel, taking big women out on the floor to dance: little men, full of grace, who could waltz their way into heaven.

Dozing in his deep-shadowed bar McGettigan has all the explanations and no answer why the singing lounges are locked up: money got tight, the drink got dear. The guards were posted at every dip in the road, waiting with the breathalyser. The booze could make no heroes.

Now his singing lounge lies like a beached whale against the gable end, a monster out of another era. Buckets on the floor to catch the leaks. The big lounge leading a point- and a pint-less existence. Mouldering away amongst fungus and falling plaster, black patches in the corners. The thin tar on the flat felt-roof taking in water, the buckled floorboards warped for the want of a damp course. The cowboy builders gone west into the sunset with so many of the travelling bands.

"Hello, Stephen. Could you get the handbrake off and fill us a pint."

A reluctant return from his noon slumber. Customers are treated with a heavy, foot-dragging indifference. The lips smacked after sleep and a dart with bent yellow plastic fins thrown wide of the board before going around to the other side of the bar, where the beermats are rationed and the crisps are out of date; and you can only hope you're not getting the first pint of the day.

Supping a slow pint in the chilly, tiled and disinfectant-smelling middle of the day. Then footfalls disturb the gravel outside. McGettigan's ears cock up like a small dog listening to the peeling of a chocolate bar wrapper, measuring the stranger's approach. The footsteps hesitate, think better of it and turn away.

You can take this level of suspense, and McGettigan watching the cartoons, only for so long. So it's out on the gritty, wind-blown street again to walk the length of the village, muzzy after a few pints, regarding the countdown to the coming bank holiday festival weekend.

The beer festivals and the beauty contests are gone: buried by the teetotallers and feminists. But the Arts Festivals and the Summer Schools have come in their place for drink and argument. At every small crossroads town there's a poster in a pub window, a string of bunting hung across the road. And if the owners are feeling particularly extravagant, a tray of sandwiches for the visitors – the sausages on the stick are reserved for the near relations.

In the village here the gables and windows are getting a lick of paint, and the pot plants are out on the sills – bedded bright blue lobelia, burning red geraniums and tumbling nasturtiums. The centre-piece is a whitethorn bush removed from a roadside ditch and planted in the middle of the pavement by the Town Improvement Committee.

Receive a bless-you wave across the way from the parish priest, Father Tim Regan, striding up the village street with his eyes fixed on the future, pulling on his pipe with a tourist steam-train head of smoke up. Grass stains on the knees of his best trousers as he heads out the hills to rage at conifers. He shakes his fist at the young saplings, and curses the ever encroaching forests of sitka spruce and lodge-pole pine – like a man beset by alien invaders in the *Day of the Triffids.*

A fresh-cut, sports-ground smoothness in the green fields between the houses in this gapped street, and the petrol engine drone of a lawnmower in the distance doing the verges coming into town. The school lawn neat as a new exercise book. An early tent pitched, pegged and rustling like a sail in the lee of a chestnut tree. The window boxes, tidy town flower tubs, painted black skillet pots and litter-bins stand regimented and waiting ... waiting ... waiting.

The local guard is out airing his State trousers. Narrowing his hungover eyes under a hard peak, Scully stretches his blue serge and Templemore training-school swung arms to ease the twinge in his wrist: permanently stiff from signing and stamping the weekly dole forms.

Every Tuesday at ten o'clock he opens the barrack's door to meet the waiting blizzard – bigger even than the great fall of forty-seven – of social security and unemployment benefit dockets that have left his stomach sour and his fingers forever stained with blue biro. For what's left of the week he tunes two diligent ears under a big blue hat to his radio link with the prowling white squad car. He types his legal reports with two accusing fingers, or sits by a loud, black telephone, taking down names in his daybook – drivers producing smudged and backdated insurance policies and an unlikely excuse from a young man with nothing on a Honda fifty only his brother. He gives out gun licences and keeps out of family rows at tinkers' weddings and funerals. Takes to his checkpoint on soft days, clears the local pubs with a shiny belt and a flashlight after a complaint of late drinking: and having his quota of names in his notebook, and

State summonses issued with satisfaction, he steps into the witness box on dinner expenses for the regular District Court, answering pin-stripe and brandy-smug solicitors, and a mumbling, reformed alcoholic District Justice no one can hear: a routine which will allow him to get his duty out of the way without rising his acid, the turf saved on the bog, and not eat into his drinking time. Then home to his barrack's bed to dream about single women and tax discs.

The hustings are up in front of the parish hall, festooned in ribbons like a new Superintendent or a politician out on polling day. Planks and scaffolding and plastic chairs waiting to seat the important. Waiting for dignitaries after a Sunday dinner to declare the festival open.

Wash-day lines of bunting made of rags have been tied between the telephone poles and the street-lamps by a handyman up on a ladder, supervised from a distance by a well-fed body of county councillors taking time off from the sheep-dipping committee. A banner offers a stencilled welcome in several tongues. Flags in county football team colours idle between yellow and white Papal flags, Italian and Irish soccer squad colours, and the sponsor's banner sagging in the middle.

Daunted by the rioting colour and the roaring daylight Guard Scully stoops through a shop door to buy another packet of twenty cigarettes.

Mrs Gillogley, village shopkeeper, with a wasp in her window, a cigarette glued to her lip and two pink bedroom slippers on her feet, tipples among her morning headache tablets, tins of Shop Local dog-food and yellow label beans. She has no change in her till for a phone call made from the public kiosk; her newpapers are gone before eleven; she's just out of bread and still waiting for the milk to come. Her tomatoes are bruised, her bananas black, her lettuce wilted, her cabbage strong, her cauliflower yellow, her scallions sad, her potatoes gone bad in the bag. She leans over an empty freezer after the ice-cream man calls, without opening the back of his van, and tells you she has no choc ices, only frozen peas.

On the same sunlit side of the street sit the old boys in open doors, with an angle on everyone that passes. Grandads minding sun-brown and pony-tailed children skimming the pavements with plastic tricycles, tractors and cut knees.

Seeing them skip past the doctor's medical dispensary you can hear again the childhood sound of rusty needles boiling in metal kidney bowls, taste the polio vaccine on a sugar cube, feel the cold of the examination couch where you sat up bare-chested and shivering under every finger tap and touch of the stethoscope. Where you fainted every time you saw those big, graduated glass syringes and ignorant needles. Then you meet with the good doctor himself, retired several years now, on his way out to the graveyard to visit his old patients.

A white spirit smell of paint about, like a parish house getting ready for the stations. A beer lorry unloading outside the best trade, if not exactly thriving, bar in the village where the publican is lifting extra glasses out of their packing. Ready for the army of schoolchildren who will fetch the glasses back to the pub when the swell of visitors carry his glassware away: abandoned on distant window-sills and ingle-nooks, or left down at street corners for fresh pints perched at unlikely angles on car bonnets.

The next pub has a desperate collection of felt-tip marker and fluorescent paper posters thumb-tacked to the door: orange, green and pink notices for monster *ceilís*, novelty events, darts and *seisiúns*, pub draws, music tonight and soup and sandwiches all day.

The cooler shelves are loaded down, the alcoves of bottles under the bar bent in the middle and brimming to the edge. And a couple of early boys are there on high stools, looking like men with no faith in the economy. Already drinking in anticipation of the weekend, impatient for something promised and glorious, something liberating and decisive to happen.

The unplanned Thursday session leaves you on an unsteady footing going into the long weekend.

The festival comes to life on Friday night, ripens to a hothouse swollen bloom on Sunday, its petals wilted or fallen by the end of the holiday Monday.

Saturday sees the visitors up at sparrow-call, looking for maps, looking for accommodation, looking for monument ruins and places to eat. Caravans and station wagons arrive, sporting German, French and Dutch national initialled stickers after the ferry crossing. Bearded and tanned young men in shorts, and leggy women burdened under rucksacks wander about. Soon there is set-dancing and rowdy drinking in the midday middle of the street. Music drifts from the workshops and the competitions. A Readymix cement lorry rolls by.

Then the farmers come in from the shorn and quilted evening meadow fields, straw-gold after the harvest. Men with the hay in and the silage covered, the turf stacked, the bulk of the summer's work done.

There was a time when the old farmers tied their coats with string in a bundle on the carrier, climbed up on their high black bicycles and pedalled to the seaside, to eat dillisk and cool their heels in salt water and seaweed baths after the summer work. Now the farmers come to the festival village instead, in rusty Japanese cars, the boots tied down with baler twine: to talk and drink out an end to Saturday night.

In the street after Sunday mass the chip-vans, ice-cream sellers and trinket stalls take up their usual places along the kerb. The festival is officially opened before a shuffling crowd as the scolding mothers chase down missing children. Then the meetings begin: bumping into all the old regulars who show up every year to go roving up and down the one street for an afternoon.

In the cool, newly whitewashed granaries and outhouses the craftspeople sit patiently by their tables; supping pints, flogging bright ear-rings to give a touch of colour to young earlobes. Alternative-minded people peeping out between dried-flower arrangements, minding spreads of wholefood and herbs, postcards and pottery, watercolours and quilted things. The big farm wives rummaging through their hand-pressed, crafted, stitched, painted and organic potted goods, looking for an old-fashioned bargain.

The crowded public houses breathe their beery invitations and the ring of traditonal music lures you from the sunlight. Burnt hay-making faces crushed three-deep at the bar, where the beer runs down to your elbows as you try to bring away a round of pints from the counter.

The bad air of the locked up singing lounges is allowed out for the weekend. In every lounge the musicians hold their corner again. Ballads rising out of lost wars and love defeated. And the onlookers raise their clerical-collared pints of Guinness to their lips, swallow and say:

"You could drink a pint like that without a word in your head."

The eyes of the flute player dance to the jig of his fingers. The man on the Uileann or "onion" pipes licks the cream of stout from his whiskers. More bearded men in bulging T-shirts beat their *bodhráns* in a drinking sweat, led by a flat-capped and long-faced fiddler wearing his best double-breasted trousers.

You push in to hear what's happening, but you can't sit still. You jostle and leave again. Looking for something. If it's not here it must be in the other pub down the street. So out you go again into the summer smells and half-light, moving with a make-believe sense of purpose through the talking people, the dashing children, the small hand-clutching infants and the little ones begging the price of chips. Past the ticket sellers and stragglers coming back bewildered from the treasure hunt; meeting uniformed men in kilts and buttoned hats out of pipe bands, drinking after the annual parade – the usual line of dwindling commercial vans, a pony and trap, wasps around your ear, three vintage cars, and the festival queen sitting on the back of a beer lorry. Oh! for a lucky meeting or a change of fate.

But all you hear is an old boy watching the young lads chatting up the German women visitors say:

"Between this Aids and the blight there won't be a stalk left in the country by September."

In the by now hopelessly muddled search after the heart of the festival weekend you find yourself missing *seisiúns* and timetabled events. You are left ticketless for the big concert, hungry for dinner but making do with villainous chips. And then you fall into the river at the children's fishing competition.

Before you know what has happened it's after one o'clock in the morning. The lights are out behind the bar, but you can still get a drink. The visitors have cleared out. The tourists are in their campers, the week-end over, their departure imminent. The girls you were talking to earlier are gone. Guard Scully is wearing a Fair Isle jumper over his official blue shirt, drinking whiskey with a farmer explaining cattle headage testing on a pro rata basis. Miss Gillogley has switched to rum and peppermint. A county councillor sings "The Rose of

Avondale" into his empty beer bottle.

With the television switched off McGettigan leans an end-of-day elbow on the bar counter. The dirty glasses can wait until the morning. He considers his tar-paper brown ceiling and his eyes glaze over thinking about bed. He dreams about a long lie-in and then someone to cook his breakfast. But he knows he will be knocked up early by some restless short-sleeper, dragged into the littered Tuesday after the festival village to sign on at the barracks. Caught with the shakes and a cold-water shave, dropping a pocketful of loose change on the bar counter, looking for the cure. He will take his time before serving and throw for that double-twenty again. A slow march around behind the counter to pull a pint and squeeze a half-one from the optic. Then he will shuffle out to clear the tables, empty the shelves and find a padlock for the bolt on the singing lounge doors to wait out another year.

Departures

OUTSIDE THE AIR-CONDITIONED TERMINAL at John F. Kennedy Airport it is a sweltering 90 degrees Fahrenheit. The air is high with aviation fuel. Sweat trickles down the back of a black baggage-handler called Pete who is filling in for me. I have shed my airport staff overalls to become another statistic in the never-ending business of departures and arrivals.

We ride the Atlantic jet-stream to Shannon in five hours. Then I pick up a rented car to take me back to the townland where I was born. It is late summer over here. The skies are grey; a white-cap of mist on the far mountain; rain in the wind; a lonesome wind in the big trees and the stormy hedgerows. And that radiance in the west, as I come around a bend in the lane into the low evening light. I had forgotten this emptiness.

The home place at the end of the lane is a slumbering vault now, rain-downs on the once white walls. The garden is a thistle-patch, the sulphur smell of nettles about the weathered stone. The cottage rose, pink lupin and dahlia beds are all gone. Only the briars and the stinging nettles took permanent root here.

I catch a bar of laughter coming across the fields. Children from the new bungalows have come out to cycle rings around the road on a shared bicycle. The younger ones take turns holding a terrier pup, wet and wriggling between bare arms, a long tongue licking ticklish ears. Boys with bicycles and wellington boots, sniffles and gap-teeth. Mirrors of my own youth, reared out of doors amongst the hawthorns and hiding places up sycamore and elm trees. Yes, I know the pattern of their hedge retreats intimately. My childhood, too, is fenced about these fields.

They watch me. The boy from the Bronx, returned to sell his past. The roadside fields of a small family farm, broken into lots and sold for sites for bungalows on the hill. New homes for neighbours' daughters, schoolgirls in my time, grown to young wives in curves of motherhood.

I have the dust of grey asphalt streets and the dusty brown ball-parks of America in my pockets. I had forgotten the natural green of this farmland: green of trees and green of hedgerows, green of meadows and pasture, green of gaps and shadows. But I remember a dancing cloud of midges caught in the last, slanting shaft of evening sunlight, the call of blackbirds in the late dusk, the damp air of enclosed paths, ticklish and threaded with wandering spider-webs. Moths on the wing at dusk in poor fields dripping with rain-water pearls.

The whole property is falling down before the forces of neglect and natural decay. I find Dutch elm disease ravaging the limbs of the old elm trees around the house, the bolts and nails of tree-houses buried deep in their seasonal rings that compass my growing years.

I take up a handful of wet grass for the earth-smell of it, and remember the very first time I heard of the city of New York and the Empire State Building. "The eighth wonder of the world," my father said, holding my small hand, walking home through the rough pasture behind a black and white milking cow.

Going around the back of the house now, past the fallen down cow-barns and roofless sheds, I take the path to the drinking well. And pushing through each summer's new growth of unchecked bindweed and ivy, I find a trickle of country lore coming back to me. Names of plants and wild flowers not seen since I left for America: fairyfingers, ox-eye daisy, saxifrage, heart's-ease, and for-get-me-not.

And I recall running in from the next meadow field, rich with the smell of seasoned hay under the sun, to bring a bottle to this same spring well. Plunging clear glass into clearer water, while the bottle bubbled and sucked up stone-cold water where it came clean out of the earth between dancing pebbles. Then running back hard in plastic sandals to bring a drink to my father. A tidy build of a man in a white shirt with the sleeves rolled up, working in a mountain meadow field long ago.

A man alive to the smell of new-mown hay on the breeze, or the horror of frogs caught on the rattling blade of the mowing machine, as the saw-teeth levelled the regular swards of June hay. Then taking out the back-sward with rakes together, working our separate ways around the border of the field.

I miss that purest satisfaction: of a clean, pale-stubbled field, with long shadows reaching out from the haycocks and hedgerows as the sun dipped behind the hills. A veil of mist rising over the still river. The far mountain, pink in the last of the light. A summer moon, low on the horizon, for that last round-up after a day of gathering, building, heading and roping the haycocks. Man and boy, working in a simpler world to an understood rhythm.

I was my own master then, picking up discarded hay-forks, waterbottles and cast-off jumpers. Closing the gaps and leaving the field at nightfall. Taking a strange pride in being the last one out.

On my way out now I find myself standing under the old sycamore tree at the road gate. I hear the drone of late-working bees amongst the mottled leaves. Seed-pods helicopter down.

I loved it best standing here in winter, late in the frosty night, when the stars glimmered more fiercely through the hard, bare branches.

Had I somehow foreseen constellations of car headlights streaming along the Franklin D. Roosevelt elevated highway? Standing at the half-way point along the boardwalk across the Brooklyn Bridge, looking through the network of steel cables at the amber- and white-lit windows of Manhattan. The floodlit crown of the Empire State Building sending shafts of red, white and blue light into a vaulted heaven. Under my feet, the ceaseless vibration of traffic, and the fretwork of these East River bridges humming the headlong song of America.

The country air comes thick with fragrant and invisible pollen. The very breath of summer. I bend towards a thicket of evening-perfumed honeysuckle. That smell, the utter quiet, the solitude, raise a familiar shiver on my back, and memories of those first, half-formed longings for travel.

I stop again where the mountain road dips towards the spangled lights of the village to study a derelict property under lonesome dales. I would not dare press my face to its clouded windows in this falling dusk. It is the home of a ghost. The ghost of a retired labourer, who told me once that in his youth he, too, had been "one of the boys from the Bronx".

When his legs could carry him about these country by-

ways no more my family had found him this place to live,
a basic shelter from the elements on the side of a mountain. A quiet, empty place, where memories of his days
labouring in the humid glare of the building sites of
America mingled freely in his imagination with the farm-
ing traditions of his youth. On a winter's evening by a
fire of turf stolen from the mountain he would confide
in me:

"I heard them last night, Sir. A *meitheal* in Barney
Kiernan's field. All night they were talking and shouting,
and I heard their shovels striking stones in them hungry
ridges."

And then he would describe for me the gangs of shirt-
less men in cloth caps and heavy boots breaking open
the heart of the Manhattan bedrock for the waves of
glimmering new skyscrapers rising against the sun-white
heavens. The rush of strange people and machines
amongst the geometric order of grid-iron city streets.
Meetings with coloured men, Chinamen wearing pony-
tails, Polish men, Jews and Italians. The foreign tongues
and foreign ways of life down in the siren-loud canyons
of Manhattan by day, and the yellow-brick tenements of
the Bronx by night.

He quit America and came here, to spend the last years
of his life in a strange no man's land, lost between Old
and New Worlds. I was a child then, rooted in a small-
farm world. And I lived in awe of his hobo life, his freedom from family chores, schoolbells and bedtimes.
When he came calling to our house I hid behind the
barns and watched him steal an egg for his supper, or a
few potatoes or vegetables out of the garden. He never
took more than he needed, and we knew that for him
the stolen bite tasted sweeter than charity.

Later I would go to his mountain shack and sit watching the old boy from the Bronx drink his tea coloured

with clotted milk from long-standing bottles in the windows. And he would spit on a black, iron frying-pan to see if it was hot enough to sizzle his fat, bristled ends of bacon and stolen onions. And then to bed, sleeping off his daily tonic of porter.

"The day I can't walk down that road for a bottle of stout, I'm done for, Sir," he told me.

Most nights the old boy from the Bronx staggered back alone and dizzy, breaking the mountain silence with regular throat-clearing coughs. He tripped one time, and rolled from the roadside ditch into the field below. I happened to come along later and I heard a familiar voice call out of the darkness:

"Are you on the road, Sir?"

"I am."

"In that case, Sir, I'm off the mark."

I take the mountain road down to the edge of the village where the community centre stands. I earned my first wage packet there, building a wall in the women's toilet. The wall sagged in the middle, but I had taken the first step of a young apprentice off that family farm on the side of the mountain. I got the first taste of builder's lime in my mouth on that job, and the first corrosive cement blisters on my fingers. And a sense of the foundations of my future life being laid out for me.

From the roof, where I spent my time with my shirt off in the sun at lunch hour, whistling at the girls going by in summer cotton, I saw the first of my neighbours calling at the local barracks to get their passport application forms stamped. That trickle became a flow, and carried most of my emigrant generation away.

On the village street, now, I meet a survivor. One of the few small farmers left up there on that lonesome mountain. One of a dying breed of black-faced bachelors. That neglected and hidden country manhood, known by the shine in their old suits, the grime along rumpled and worn shirt collars and cuffs, the burnt-yellow nicotine-coloured fingers and nails and the yesterday shave. That telling black in the pores: the mark of men who no longer wash, no longer care, all hope of greater fulfilment grizzled and weathered away.

He could be the last inhabitant on the planet; a bachelor until he dies. For women are hard to come by, up there amongst the short grass, wet rocks and low rainclouds. But he knows where he belongs. Stepping easy in a patchwork of old suits, flat cap down over his ears, his long coat belted about a thin frame, walking a narrow black bicycle for company.

Watching his even-paced progress in this empty street I find it hard to believe that in forty-eight hours from now I will be standing on the Grand Concourse at Fordham in the Bronx again, watching the evening traffic grinding through the smoke-hot dusk after a day of big summer heat. Then taking a downtown train under crowded Manhattan streets and crossing into Brooklyn, where it will be a muggy eighty-two degrees down on Montague Street. The neighbourhood streets will belong to strolling couples, big men with bill-folds lying fat on the hip, cinnamon-skinned youths loafing or jostling on the corners and the car fenders. And I will stop for a couple of chilled beers and shoot a game of pool, before going on to weekend work in the alien glare of a gas-station forecourt.

The old boy props his bicycle against a rusty petrol pump. We step over a sheepdog lying across the pub door and we go in together.

There are groceries at the top end of the bar counter, the bare essentials for drinking men: tins of corned beef, sardines in oil, loaves of bread and half-pounds of butter, and strong, untipped cigarettes. Bachelor's provisions.

After the brash, self-conscious bars of the Bronx this is a den of empty shadows, silent men and old upholstery. The men consider their bottled stout and half-ones. Welcomes are muted as I settle into the curious comfort of my own kind.

I shout a drink for the old boy who came in with me. He takes a bottled beer and asks:

"What do you make of life over there in the States, anyway?"

And I tell him.

"Sometimes I think I've wandered off the mark."

FICTION TITLES FROM BRANDON

MICHAEL JOE, A Novel of Irish Life
William Cotter Murray

"Michael Joe is a shopkeeper in a small Irish town. He's bitterly submissive to Mother and Church. Lusting after girls. Cocky about football prowess. Muddled by drink, vanity and jealousy. Mr Murray conveys a human history and view of Irish life with the quicksilver words of a story-teller."
New York Times

"Mr Murray has recollected... a small town in County Clare, re-created it with the most vivid accuracy and populated it with authentic life... [He] has fashioned a book which entitles him to rank with the best of Ireland's novelists."
Augustine Martin

"A triumph of objectivity and unspoken judgment... The story is perfectly observed."
Virginia Kirkus

320 pages; ISBN 0 86322 128 9; paperback £5.99

BALLYBAWN
Padraig J. Higgins

Under the influence of a potion used usually to strengthen stallions, Garda Muldoon disgraces himself and his uniform and is dismissed from the force. Sergeant O'Reilly, his prospects of promotion ruined, announces to the village of Ballybawn that the police are now on strike and takes himself and his young colleague off on pilgrimage to Lourdes.

"Higgins's first novel is firmly in the fantastical satirical tradition of Flann O'Brien... likely to become a cult book among malcontents." *Irish Press*

224 pages; ISBN 0 86322 127 0; paperback £5.99

THE DEVIL'S CARD
Mary Maher

"Mary Maher's powerful, gripping novel... is both a murder mystery and a political thriller." *The Irish Times*

"Engrossing... *The Devil's Card* is a fine achievement and deserves a wide readership. Its tale of corruption in high places has parallels with our own time." *Sunday Press*

"*The Devil's Card* is a warm and intelligent exploration of Irish-America. It is both sympathetic and admirably unsentimental." *Sunday Tribune*

"As historical events go, this is a rare gem, well worth retelling. And if you like your fiction factional, *The Devil's Card* is hard to beat. *Writers' Monthly*

288 pages; ISBN 0 86322 130 0; hardback £12.99

KILBRONEY
Kathleen O'Farrell

The Mountains of Mourne provide the dramatic setting for this enthralling story of passion and conflict. The year is 1780, a time of uneasy peace and simmering tension. Against the backdrop of conflict between landlord and tenant, and between England and France, an intense personal drama is acted out.

"A beautifully written book with a cornucopia of historical details so seamlessly woven through the fabric of the narrative." *Newry Reporter*

352 pages; ISBN 0 86322 141 6; paperback; £5.99

942670 — Paula
                    +
Asfa + Kamal   Pat
5 The Furrows
Walton on Thames
0932 220916